Diamonds, Dinner Jackets, and Death

....

Steve Higgs

This book is dedicated to Libby Bolin from California who won the 'Suggest a Title' competition. Thank you, Libby.

Contents

Kidnapped

From the window of my limousine, the busy streets of London flashed by. Filled with people going about their lives, the streets were wet with drizzle as the English weather did what it does best. As the driver paused in traffic, I put my phone back into my handbag; we were nearly there.

To my right was Green Park, one of many open spaces in the nation's capital, and just ahead was the Ritz. I'd stayed there once before, many years ago when I would have claimed to be happily married. That marriage was ancient history even if the divorce was only just getting under way, but I remembered the hotel as a romantic and beautiful place to visit or stay.

We were staying there as guests of the Maharaja of Zangrabar, the third richest man on the planet and someone I could refer to as a personal friend. A while back I stumbled across a giant sapphire that belonged to his family. It was a prized jewel of their nation and a symbol of the country's prosperity that had been stolen by an American thief thirty years earlier.

With the help of some friends, I returned it, got a healthy reward, and an invitation to attend the new Maharaja's coronation. It was there that I met the Maharaja, but only after foiling a plot by his uncle to steal the throne out from under him. Now I live in a huge house which he gifted to me and, on my way back to the ship where this whole adventure started, I am stopping off to attend a banquet which he has thrown to honour the recent peace between Zangrabar and its northern neighbour Itarnia.

The Maharaja's invitation told me we would be staying at the Ritz, but the cars he sent for us drove straight past the famous old hotel without stopping. The driver saw me swing my head around to stare at the hotel vanishing behind the car and then saw the question forming on my lips.

With a smile of reassurance, he said, 'The Maharaja has arranged the banquet to be held at a secret location, Mrs Fisher.'

'Where?' I demanded, fear forming a ball in the pit of my belly as Agent Wayne Garrett, a policeman from Scotland Yard assigned to be my bodyguard, also began to get excited.

'Hey!' he shouted. 'The lady asked you a question.'

'Nearly there,' the driver replied jovially and turned on his indicator. He was speaking to us from the front of the car through an intercom because the two parts of the stretched limousine were divided by a glass partition.

I swung my head around again to look out of the rear window, gripping my dachshunds Anna and Georgie tightly to me for comfort. If I was getting kidnapped, so too were my friends as they followed in the car behind. I was here, and had a police bodyguard, only because I was on the run from the head of an underworld organised crime firm. The head of the firm, a shadowy figure known only as the Godmother, wanted me dead because I'd unwittingly ruined her plans more than once. As my panic rose, I couldn't stop myself from laughing at the irony of getting kidnapped as I try to run away.

The driver flicked his indicator on and turned down a narrow side street. I peered through the window, trying to catch the name of the road, but missed it as the car drove onwards. Wayne had his hand inside his jacket on the holster of his sidearm where it twitched with indecision. Shooting out the glass to get to the driver was a fairly extreme step to take, but when the driver turned the wheel to coax the long vehicle down a ramp and underneath a building, we both sensed it was time to act.

As Wayne began to draw his gun, I grabbed his arm and yelled, 'Wait!' I stared through the glass partition and out of the windscreen for a heartbeat as I made sure my eyes were not being deceived. But I had it right: The Maharaja's personal valet, Aladdin Alshaibi, was ahead of us with a squad of Zangrabar's royal guard behind him. 'Oh, thank goodness,' I gasped.

'Mrs Fisher?' Wayne prompted. He was ready to act and impatient to do something.

'It's okay. I don't know where we are, but I know who that is.' I pointed to Aladdin.

The driver slowed the car, bringing it to a gentle stop whereupon the royal guard stepped forward to open the doors on both sides simultaneously.

Aladdin beamed a wide smile. 'Welcome to the Exclusive, Mrs Fisher.'

Seeing the trepidation on our faces as he led us toward the opaque doors, Aladdin attempted to reassure us. 'Please have no concern, honoured guests. The Exclusive has long been the retreat of the world's most wealthy and it is one of the safest places on the planet. The Maharaja chose this hotel specifically because it is so safe. No one is allowed to bring any weapons inside, and the hotel has a well-trained security team who carry only non-lethal weapons. For these reasons, it is the perfect place for meeting between parties with ... quarrelsome pasts.'

My live-in gym instructor friend, Barbie, my butler, Jermaine, and Molly, the housemaid, had all been travelling in the second car. From their wide eyes, they had also met the unannounced and sudden change of destination with shock and worry, but seeing my relaxed posture, Barbie gave me a smile.

'I wondered what was going on, Patty,' she jabbered, as she often did when nerves got the better of her. 'I thought it might be the Godmother again.'

'As did I,' I admitted.

She gave the dogs a quick scratch behind their ears and looked at the inviting lobby area ahead of us. The hotel staff were waiting patiently for us to walk inside, while yet more of them were taking our luggage from the cars.

When more cars appeared, gliding down the ramp into the mysterious underground front lobby, it was clearly time to get inside.

However, getting inside was not exactly complicated, but it was nothing like arriving at a normal hotel. To start with, the entrance is via an underground car park and then we had to go through a metal detector because they needed to be sure we had no weapons. The staff were lovely; all smiles and warm greetings as they professionally dealt with us. Agent Garrett was not happy about surrendering his weapon, but gave it up when he accepted he wasn't getting in without doing so.

They had too many high value targets the head of security explained. Lena Glauser, a tall blonde woman in her early forties, oversaw the operation in the reception lobby with military precision.

'Where is your accent from?' I asked her, curious because it wasn't one I could place. It sounded almost German, but I didn't think it was.

'I grew up in Interlaken in Switzerland,' she replied, and it was then that I noticed the Swiss flag on the wall behind her.

Tracking my eyes, Aladdin said, 'This is Swiss soil, Mrs Fisher. There are three of these exclusive hotels. One in Washington DC, one in Beijing, and this one here in London. Each of them is operated by the Swiss government and is considered to be Swiss soil much the same way as an embassy retains the sovereignty of its home nation. They are politically neutral which makes them a perfect place to host events such as the Maharaja's banquet.'

Once Wayne was suitably disarmed and we were checked in, a team of staff took our luggage and escorted us to our suites on the fourth floor. There were twelve floors in total, the topmost of which was dedicated to a single residence. I couldn't imagine what the price tag to rent it for one night might be, but I was willing to bet there were small countries on the planet that wouldn't make that much in a year.

Aladdin explained all this as he escorted us to our suites.

My eyes were agog at the interior decoration which was luxury and elegance on a scale I had never seen before. My friends were doing exactly the same, most notably Molly, the nineteen-year-old maid/cleaner who was already employed at the house when I took residence. She had the same ordinary life ninety-nine percent of the population enjoy, and though she worked in a grand house, I don't think she could imagine what she now bore witness to.

I invited her along on this trip to ensure the Godmother couldn't target her and even said she could bring her boyfriend. She elected to dump him instead, explaining that he wasn't much good as a boyfriend and she could get a new one. Barbie also left her lover behind. Hideki, a junior doctor from Japan now working in London, could not come with us without jeopardising his career, so he moved in with a colleague close to the hospital. Barbie wasn't happy about leaving him behind, but there really wasn't any choice. I hoped to reunite them soon.

Jermaine also split from his lover, but in his case, he was the one who got dumped when his boyfriend announced he had no intention of waiting around. Of course, he did not reveal this news, Barbie did, but confided that he had been stoical about the split since it clearly wasn't meant to be.

All this ran through my head as I thought about my own situation. I had one love interest here at the banquet tonight. David

Sebastian is the Lord Mayor of Kent and quite a catch. The biggest problem when I consider him was that I hadn't cast a net. Additionally, I had a potentially nasty divorce hanging over my head and furthermore, waiting for me aboard the cruise ship, Aurelia, our next destination after the banquet, was Captain Alistair Huntley, a former lover impatient to resume our relationship.

It was a lot to think about.

Divorce

If you think the Ritz is grand or plush, or you have ever stayed in a place that you thought of as luxurious and opulent, then let me tell you, it has nothing on our secret accommodation. Our driver used the term secret when he referred to the hotel and he wasn't kidding. The hotel doesn't even have a name displayed outside, it doesn't have a website, there is no ornate frontage to it, and they don't advertise. It looks like nothing until you get inside, and then you discover a palace of opulence. It is the type of place millionaires cannot afford to stay in and probably don't even know about. In order to come here, one needed billions. Several of them.

Once in our rooms, we were left to relax and unwind. The rooms, of course, were all enormous suites with giant bath-tubs, grand views over the city, and every luxury a person might be able to perceive. Honestly, I was surprised the bath-room sink didn't have a third tap that dispensed gin, fitted specially for my arrival.

Barbie had her own suite, but together with Molly, we chose to have a girly pamper session together in mine. Masseuses had beaten our muscles into submission, and then we endured the rigours of multiple skin and hair treatments before succumbing to the temptation of professional makeup artists who made me look ten years younger somehow.

All that kept the three of us occupied for the last three hours, eating away the afternoon so now it was early evening and getting dark outside. The banquet was due to start at eight o'clock, and a good thing too because I was already getting hungry. We were all wearing thick, fluffy white monogrammed bathrobes and fluffy white mule slippers. I wanted to leave my ballgown until the last moment. I had it made specially for the occasion, and at a rush because we only got a few days' notice. The price tag had been eye-watering, but I thought I looked good in it; the best I had looked in many years, yet I was also terrified of putting it on in case anything happened to it.

Ten minutes ago, lost in my blissful cloud, I answered my phone without first thinking to check who the caller was and had been arguing with my husband ever since. I sighed as I attempted to explain things for the third time. 'Charlie, it really doesn't matter what you attempt to threaten me with. I will not be attending the preliminary meeting your solicitor has arranged. There was no need for you to call me.'

'So you propose to only speak to me through your lawyer now, is that it?' my soon-to-be-ex-husband snapped.

Patiently, I phrased my reply. 'Charlie, it was not I who hired a lawyer to begin this process. I would have split our assets amicably. In fact, I was quite prepared to let you have the house and the cars and even the money you so deftly squir-relled away throughout our marriage.' He had no clever reply. 'If you did not now believe that you have some claim to my current assets, those gained since we split, then it would not be necessary to speak through our individual legal counsels.'

'My claim is completely legitimate, Patricia. I seek only an even split; the very thing you asked for. You think it incon-venient now that you have vastly more than me, but the deal stands, and a fifty-fifty split is common among married per-sons of our age.'

'You won't get a penny of the Maharaja's money, Charlie, and I will not be at the meeting.'

'Well, you have to attend the meeting, Patricia,' Charlie insist-ed as if that would make any difference.

For years I tolerated his bullying, meekly bowing down to his demands and playing the role of obedient wife. Right now, I couldn't imagine what might have been in my mind, but the timid woman he preferred was long gone.

'My lawyer has cancelled the meeting, Charlie. There no longer is a meeting and your lawyer cannot proceed with anything until I return. The only thing you achieve with this nonsense is the emptying of your bank account as your lawyer charges you by the hour, and for every communication he sends.'

There was a sense of wry amusement in his voice when he said, 'I consider it to be money well spent.'

I wanted to wring his neck. The phone conversation was over. I was going to hang up and berated myself for answering it in the first place. I wouldn't make that mistake again.

'Goodbye, Charlie. Please do not call me again unless you have abandoned this ridiculous quest.'

As I moved the phone away from my ear, he called out to stop me, 'Wait!'

Angry at myself for not stabbing the red button to end the call, I asked, 'What is it, Charlie?'

'Where are you going to be that you cannot rearrange the meeting? My lawyer said you were going to be away for an undisclosed amount of time.'

I thought about how I wanted to answer his question and couldn't stop the smile creeping onto my face when I said, 'Goodbye, Charlie.' This time I did hit the button, cutting him off with a promise to myself that I would never answer his calls again.

'Patty, you are a lot more polite than I would be,' said Barbie. 'Is he really trying to get half of the Maharaja's house and everything that goes with it?'

I nodded my head when really I ought to be shaking it in disbelief. 'That is what his lawyer thinks he can get. At some point when I briefly stayed with him, just before you and Jermaine arrived, I demanded we split everything down the middle. He was horrified at the time, but a day later I got the Maharaja's house and now he thinks we should stick with the deal.'

Barbie scowled. 'He is not very nice.'

I snorted a laugh. On my lap, Georgie, my miniature dachshund puppy, awoke briefly, squirmed, and went back to sleep. Next to me, her mother, Anna slept on her back, her fangs showing as her jowls flopped back with gravity. I patted them both and looked up at my friend. 'I have another word for him. Several in fact and none of them should ever be said in church.'

That brought a smile to her face. 'Champagne?' she asked, eyeing the bottle chilling on the table.

Jermaine appeared as if by magic the moment Barbie mentioned the champagne. My butler, a tall, muscular Jamaican man who fakes a British accent after watching all the episodes of Downton Abbey, was at my beck and call, not because he was paid to fulfil that role, but because he wanted to be.

'Shall I open this, madam?' he asked, taking the near-freezing bottle of ludicrously expensive champagne from the ice bucket.

We didn't need to go down for an hour, and I had abstained all afternoon even though it seemed like a perfectly reasonable time to indulge. Right now, I could not for the life of me, come up with a reason to resist any longer.

'Yes, please, Jermaine,' I replied with a smile. 'As long as you are joining us.' He let a grin crease his face; he'd been expecting this. 'You are not my butler tonight, Jermaine. Nor do you ever have to be.' I held up a hand to stop him as he opened his mouth to argue. 'I know, sweetie; it is what you want to do. I'm just saying that you don't have to, and I certainly don't need you playing butler tonight at the banquet. You will sit to my left and enjoy yourself. I insist.'

'Very, good, madam,' he conceded, letting the cork go with a pop.

'Whoo!' cheered Barbie.

'Cor, I've never had real champagne,' said Molly, her teenage eyes wide. 'My boyfriend buys the cheap, fizzy stuff from the supermarket sometimes when he wants to get me drunk.'

Expert at such things, Jermaine spilled not one drop as a fifth person joined us. Warren Garrett was a police officer with a special organised crime division at Scotland Yard. He'd been assigned to me as personal protection because of the Godmother and a shadowy organisation she ran called the Alliance of Families. They were a sort of super-umbrella firm operating above the organised crime families to control and direct their activities. The Godmother wanted me dead badly enough that she had already sent teams of assassins to do the job. Obviously, they hadn't succeeded yet, but for public safety as much as anything else, I was now in hiding and on my way to join a cruise ship. Agent Garrett was to keep me alive, but secretly I believed his mission was to be ready to learn something when the Godmother struck. The police wanted to catch her, and her organisation, but had few leads. That made me of high value to them if they could use me as bait.

Of course, I might just be a little paranoid.

'Why is it sparkling like that?' asked Barbie, holding her glass up to the light and peering through it with her giant doe eyes.

Molly, a short woman at barely over five feet and petite like a child still even though she was nineteen, held her glass up just like Barbie and came to stand next to her, mimicking the older woman's movements. 'Is that not normal then?'

Before Barbie could answer, Jermaine said, 'The sparkles are diamond dust.' All three of us stared at him, and Wayne moved in behind Jermaine to look at the bottle. 'What you are about to drink is the world's most expensive production champagne.'

'How much is it a bottle?' asked Molly, taking a sip.

'Two hundred thousand pounds,' said Jermaine.

Molly spat her mouthful out in shock, then looked mortified because there was enough to buy a Mercedes now on the carpet and dripping off her button nose.

I was less surprised, but still a little shocked by the price tag. The bottle arrived an hour ago, compliments of the Maharaja who was yet to put in an appearance. We were his special guests, but he'd rented out the entire hotel for the weekend and filled it with special guests, so I wasn't expecting to get to spend much time in his company.

I lifted my glass to take a sip and see if it could possibly be worth the money, but a scream ripped through the air to stall my arm.

Everyone froze, just for a moment, as the scream's echoes died away.

Then Jermaine and Wayne were moving, fast feet carrying them to the door with Barbie and I hot on their heels. Poor

Molly just looked stunned and probably wondered why we were all running towards the screaming and not away.

Bursting from the door and into the wide, high, and opulent hallway outside, we were faced with an obvious open door. Still wearing our bathrobes, neither Barbie nor I paused for a second as we ran after the men and in through the open door opposite.

A second scream, this one in surprise to the men running toward her, was cut off when Wayne produced his police identification. Coming down a short hallway behind Jermaine and Barbie, I couldn't see who he was talking to, but Wayne was taking charge.

'Stand back, please, Miss,' he instructed someone I couldn't see. A second later, I got to the end of the hallway and came into the suite's main room. This suite mirrored mine exactly, with one small difference: there was no dead body in mine.

The Ambassador is Dead

- -

In the middle of the suite's central room, a man lay face down in a pool of blood. There was enough blood for me to consider checking his pulse to be pointless. Six feet from him was one of the hotel's staff, a woman in her late twenties wearing the same uniform as the person who delivered our champagne earlier. She had no colour in her face and wore a look of abject terror.

Jermaine went to her, backing the startled-looking woman toward a chair so she could sit before she fell. I heard him giving words of comfort, but my feet were drawn toward the victim. He was face down and facing away from us, forcing me to walk around the room to get a look at his face. I didn't recognise him, yet I worried he might be someone important.

The man wore a dinner jacket and bow tie ready for the gala dinner tonight. His skin tone and features told me he was from the Middle East. He had young features, though his jet-black hair was shot through with grey turning to white and I guessed his age to be somewhere in his sixties. He would be from Itarnia or Zangrabar, one or the other, and a death among the members of either delegation could be nothing but bad news.

His sightless eyes answered the question about his condition, but Wayne moved in to check his pulse anyway.

I turned to the member of hotel staff. 'Whose room is this, please?' Her head twitched to look in my direction, but no answer came, and she looked too stunned to form a sentence. I tried a different approach, crossing the room to get closer, I knelt next to Jermaine. 'What's your name?'

'Andrea Eggenberger,' she managed, the simpler question generating an automatic response.

Using a gentle tone, I asked, 'Andrea, who is that man?'

She swallowed hard. 'I didn't do it.' Her eyes began to widen as concern that she might be blamed gripped her. 'It wasn't me! I just found him like that!'

I tried to calm her. 'Shhh, shhh, now, Andrea. No one is accusing you of anything. Why don't you tell me what happened?'

She looked ready to bolt; we were crowding her, and she was already frightened. 'I, ah, I need to go.'

She tried to move toward the door, but Jermaine blocked her path. 'I'm sorry, Miss Eggenberger, it would be inappropriate for you to leave at this time. We must call hotel security and treat this as a crime scene.'

'I didn't do it,' she repeated.

Wayne tapped my shoulder. 'We should all leave the room, Mrs Fisher. This *is* a crime scene. I need to check the other rooms in this suite to make sure this is the only body and see if anyone else is here. Please do not touch anything. That goes for you too, Miss,' Wayne said sternly, making sure Andrea got the message. 'Call security from another room, do not touch the phone in here.'

It was decidedly different to have a police officer around. More usually, when we find a body, we have to do everything ourselves, sometimes while being chased or shot at by the killer.

I started to move toward the door, holding my hand out for Andrea to follow us. I didn't get more than about five feet though before people appeared outside the still-open door. I recognised their uniforms as members of the Zangrabar Royal Guard – the Maharaja's personal guard. They fanned out on either side of the door, creating a human funnel from which the Maharaja himself appeared.

His confident strides faltered when he saw me, and I, in turn, ground to a halt as I found myself facing a king. He looked unchanged since the last time I saw him, though perhaps just a little taller and a little broader at the shoulder. He'd turned seventeen just a month ago, I knew that much, but despite his intelligence and maturity, he was still so young to be the ruler of an entire nation.

The Maharaja recovered swiftly, murmuring something to an aide at his side before greeting me with a smile. 'Mrs Fisher it's so wonderful to see you again. I see you have met tonight's guest of honour, the Itarnian Ambassador.'

Horror gripped me as I realised who the dead man had to be. This was the ambassador's suite and the Maharaja was here to greet him in person. Perhaps he intended to escort him down to the banquet, a sign to everyone that the two countries' troubled past was now just that.

I sucked in a shuddering breath and pulled myself upright - a person shouldn't slouch in the company of a king – even if one is only wearing a bathrobe and knickers - then I nodded my head in a small bow and said, 'Your Majesty. It thrills me to see you again, yet it pains me that I must greet you with grave news.' The Maharaja's head tilted to one side in question. 'I'm afraid the ambassador has been murdered.'

'What!' The young king darted forward, leaving his escort guard behind. They rushed to follow, bouncing off each other in the narrow hallway in their bid to keep their king safe, but there was no danger, just the horror that awaited them in the suite's central space.

As he reached the end of the hallway and came into the room, the Maharaja's feet slowed. None of us had touched the body, save for Wayne when he checked the man's pulse, so he was still lying face down in a pool of his own blood. Andrea was out of the chair Jermaine backed her into but only two feet from it and looking every bit as panicked as she had before.

'He is dead?' The Maharaja sought to confirm.

Wayne nodded his head. 'I'm afraid so, sir. I checked for signs of life myself.' When the king flicked his eyes to look at Wayne, the policeman produced his identification. 'Agent Wayne Garrett. I'm Mrs Fisher's bodyguard.'

Curious, the Maharaja looked at Jermaine. 'I thought Mr Clarke performed that role?'

A wry smile made it to my face. 'My circumstances have changed, Your Highness. If there is time, I can explain later. Is that the ambassador?' I enquired, meaning the obvious body lying on the carpet.

The Maharaja nodded his head slowly. 'Yes, I'm afraid so. This is terrible.' Catching himself before he said something he shouldn't, he snapped his head around to look at Aladdin. 'Clear the room. Essential personnel only. We need to take care of this swiftly.'

Wayne stepped forward. 'I'm afraid not, sir. This is a murder investigation now. I will summon the police and control things here until I am relieved. Please exit the room along with the rest of your men.'

Not used to being given orders, the Maharaja could have reacted any number of ways, yet he remained calm when he replied. 'I believe you are not aware of the situation you find yourself in, Agent Garrett. You are not currently in England and as such neither you, nor your police have any jurisdiction here.'

I face-palmed. 'Of course. This hotel is owned and operated by the Swiss government and the land it is on is designated at Swiss soil. Much like entering an embassy, we are now in Switzerland.'

Zangrabar's ruler turned back to address Wayne again. 'I would ask that you remain, Agent Garrett. I may have use of your skills and knowledge if you are willing. This murder may have significant repercussions for my country, and for the ambassador's. This is no murder. This is an assassination.'

His claim made half the people in the room gasp in shock.

The Maharaja looked sad when he explained. 'The recently brokered peace between our two countries is resting on a knife edge. Our wounds are not forgotten, so while the rulers can shake hands and put the past behind us, the villagers near the borders continue to snipe at each other. If the Itarnians believe their ambassador was murdered by a Zangrabarian, it will lead to war.' As an idea suddenly occurred to him, he spun around to face me and gripped both my shoulders. 'Mrs Fisher, I have no right to ask anything of you. The world knows I owe you my life and my throne already, but I must beg that you turn that brain of yours to solving this crime.'

His passion startled me, and I could find no appropriate response.

Before I could find the words, he pressed me to say yes. 'It would be no exaggeration to claim that many thousands of lives rest upon the outcome, Mrs Fisher. I need to know who killed the ambassador. I dread to think one of my own countrymen could have performed such a misguided act, but I must know, Mrs Fisher. Will you come to my aid one more time?' Then he fell to his knees and held my hand, begging me to be his detective for the sake of his nation.

Not that I planned to, but how could anyone say no to that?

Seeing his king act in such a humble manner, Aladdin dropped to his knees too. It caused a ripple effect as all the royal guard followed suit and soon I was surrounded by men on their knees while a king held my hand and waited for my answer.

I felt like throwing up.

Barbie nudged me and hissed, 'Say something, Patty.'

Finding my tongue while my head swam with overwhelming emotions, I managed to blurt, 'Yes. Yes, of course, Your Highness. You owe me nothing. I am the one who owes you. I will do whatever I can and find the killer if I am able.'

Looking overwhelmed with relief, the Maharaja bounced back to his feet, Aladdin and the guards copied him, but I was still in the spotlight. 'Whatever resources you need, Aladdin will provide.' He turned to his valet. 'Please avail yourself to Mrs Fisher this night, Aladdin. Ensure that she is given anything she asks for.'

Aladdin bowed deeply. 'Yes, Your Highness. It will be done. What of the general, Majesty?'

'The general?' I echoed.

As the captain of the guard began to shoo his soldiers from the room, the young Maharaja bowed his head and looked flustered for the first time. A frown creased his handsome features where the beginning of a beard was forming. 'I think we can expect the general to be a problem.' Sensing that I didn't know to whom he was referring, he looked up again. 'General Akbar Armand is the head of their Itarnian forces. Reze Farshad, the Itarnian Prime Minister, sent him to attend the banquet tonight. It is supposed to be a demonstration of unity; the head of my forces and the head of theirs, eating at the same table after so many decades of fighting. There are to be TV cameras here to record it, but if the general gets wind that the ambassador is dead, he will declare it to be an attack by my troops and most likely demand war. He has a lot of support in his country, a good percentage of his countrymen want to continue fighting. If he staged a coup, I'm not sure he would lose.'

The situation was far more grave than I knew.

'He is waiting downstairs for me to return with Ambassador Hosseini. I came to collect him as he is my guest of honour tonight. He is to sit to my left while we dine. When I return without the ambassador, General Armand will become suspicious. It is in his nature.' A small sigh escaped his lips. 'I must face the music, as they say.'

'Your Highness, wait,' I was having radical ideas. 'Is it necessary to tell him straight away? If you think he will react so badly, can you give me some time to determine who the killer might be? Perhaps this was one of the general's men.'

The idea that the general might create the reason to renew hostilities hadn't occurred to the teenage king. 'That is an intriguing thought, Mrs Fisher. He would have more to gain than most. The ambassador being killed at an event I myself am hosting ... yes, I can see how that might fit. It would be quite the thing to accuse him though. I must have iron-clad proof, Mrs Fisher. Can you do that?'

I raised both hands to slow him down. 'I just suggested that it could be one of his men. At this point, it could be anyone.

All I am saying is that the banquet could proceed without the ambassador. You could say that he is feeling ill,' I suggested

The Maharaja pursed his lips and gave it some thought. 'I believe he will come here to check for himself.'

I didn't have an immediate answer for that problem. 'We may have to hope that he does not, but perhaps we will be able to construct a ruse that will put him off the scent.' It wouldn't be the first time my friends and I had to act a role to get the job done.

I exchanged a glance with Barbie, and she glanced down with an icky face at the dead body still lying in a pool of its own blood. 'I'm sure we'll come up with something. We'll need to stay in here for a while now, won't we? I mean, someone's going to have to turn him over and see if there is a knife or something still sticking out of him.'

Upon hearing that, Wayne pushed off the sideboard he'd been resting against. 'I've been demoted to civilian it seems, but I can still be of use.' With a nod at Jermaine to ask for help, the two men grasped shoulders and ankles and turned the poor ambassador over, so he rested on his back. I noted rigour was beginning to set in, which made his death at least two hours old, if not more.

Aladdin made a small sound to draw the Maharaja's attention. 'Your Highness, your guests await.'

Thoughtfully, the king took a deep breath. 'I am truly sorry for this terrible imposition, Mrs Fisher. I invited you here so that I might enjoy your company and host you, and yet I find it necessary to burden you with a terrible task. I wish you luck and a swift result.'

He gave a final bow of his head and left the room.

No one spoke for a moment. I think we were all rather stunned, but the body demanded attention. Conscious that I was still clad in my bathrobe and needed to get dressed, I nevertheless put the task off for a few minutes more so I could examine the ambassador.

There was no obvious hilt of a knife sticking from his ribcage, so the source of the blood and cause of his death therefore demanded a closer inspection. Had he been shot? Was it a stabbing? I needed information and as much of it as I could get because I was against the clock like never before.

'Wayne do you have any gloves with you?' I asked, hoping the policeman might carry such things as part of his permanent arsenal.

'What? Oh, yes.' He began digging in an inside jacket pocket. 'You want me to have a look at the wound, yes?'

'Yes, please.'

Footsteps behind me made me look just as Aladdin came back into the suite. He bowed his head and was about to speak when I held up a finger to stop him. 'You're not about to start with all the eminence rubbish, are you, Aladdin? You can address me as Patricia, or Mrs Fisher if you really must.'

He dipped his head again and smiled. 'Very good, Mrs Fisher. Is there anything I can do to be of assistance?'

I switched my attention back to the ambassador as Wayne unbuttoned first his jacket and then his shirt. He had to reach over to avoid getting his feet or anything else in the pool of blood. 'Not yet, Aladdin. I'll let you know.'

'Can I go yet?' asked Andrea. She'd recovered from the terrible shock and her colour was back, but she didn't want to be here any more than I did.

'Stabbed,' concluded Wayne once he had the shirt open. He pointed to the wound. 'You can tell what sort of knife it was by the shape of the incision. It looks like a stiletto blade to me. Double-sided and designed for plunging between ribs.'

Andrea said, 'Ewww,' and gagged. 'I really need to leave now.'

I had no right to detain her. None of us did, but I needed to know what, if anything, she knew. 'Let's go to my suite instead,' I suggested. 'I need to find some clothes, and you look like you could do with a drink, Andrea.' She genuinely did, but I was using it as bait to get her to come with me.

'I'll get dressed too, then come to find you,' said Barbie, turning left as she left the ambassador's room. Jermaine came with me; he was already dressed in his dinner jacket though I wondered if he might now change given the altered plan for the evening.

We left Wayne behind to stay with the body. He was examining it and checking the ambassador's pockets plus having a sweep around the suite to see if there was anything obviously missing.

What was missing wasn't obvious.

Hidden Talents

B ack in my suite, Anna and Georgie bounded out to greet me, their little tails wagging like mad. Georgie's age could still be measured in weeks, so I prudently checked the rooms for accidents. I found none, thankfully. I travelled with a portable indoor doggy toilet which Anna had learned to use, but Georgie was too young to understand.

Molly was nowhere in sight. Deciding that she had most likely gone back to her own suite, I asked Jermaine to mix gin and tonic for everyone and ran to my bedroom to change. Hanging from a door was my ballgown, a floor-length item made from silk and designed to hug my figure where I was happy for it to, and be a little kinder where I wanted a part of me to be hidden. I would be wearing a corset beneath it to flatten my tummy – an area I would never be able to truly flatten with exercise – but I wasn't putting it on to solve a murder. It was no good for crime-solving, so it went back in the wardrobe, replaced by a pair of snug jeans, flat court shoes, a white silk top, and a deep-blue Chanel jacket which I'd bought as a treat when I took the money from my first ever paid case.

Now, my detective business was going sour because I wasn't there to answer calls or take cases. I had taken down the adverts and website already. I had no choice other than to run away but I was going home as soon as I could and would pick up where I'd been forced to leave off.

Andrea's glass was empty by the time I got back to the central living area of my suite. She was curled up with her feet tucked under her on one of the couches, still looking a little shell-shocked.

Jermaine brought a glass to me, which I accepted gratefully. 'I have arranged for food as well, madam. The kitchen staff were very accommodating. Hotel security have arrived as well. They are in the ambassador's suite with Mr Garrett.'

'Very, good. Thank you, Jermaine.' I took a gulp of gin, savouring the heady botanicals. 'I will speak with them shortly. When Barbie returns, the three of us should have a cramming session and see what we can figure out.' I sat myself opposite Andrea.

Suddenly self-conscious, she swung her legs back down to take her feet off the couch. 'Sorry,' she said, looking guilty.

I waved a dismissive hand. 'You've had quite a shock, Andrea. Can you tell me why you were in the ambassador's suite? Was the door open when you got to it?' I wanted to know how she came to find the body. Hotel staff would come to the door if delivering something, they would have keys though and be able to get in if they chose to.

'I was sent to clean the room,' she told me. 'Someone in the room called down to report the room was in need of a tidy and had some dirty plates to be taken away. I was sent to deal with it. The door was locked, so I knocked, got no answer, and let myself in. I called out again once I was inside and still got no answer and I suppose you heard me scream when I found the man. Did you say he is an ambassador?'

I nodded rather than answer, deep in thought already. 'What else can you tell me, Andrea?'

'Um,' she replied, my question had been quite broad.

'How about the call to get someone to clean the room. Was it a male voice? Are such phone calls recorded ever?'

Andrea didn't know. 'I don't answer the calls. That's done in the control room and I don't think they are recorded.'

They must be logged though, I told myself, hoping we would be able to speak to the person who took the call. 'Was there anyone in the hallway when you came to the ambassador's suite? Did you see anyone at all, maybe waiting to get into the elevator when you came out of it?'

She gave her head a vigorous shake. 'No, no, I didn't see anyone.' I'm sure she intended to mask it, but her reaction came across as false. I believed she had just lied to me.

A knock at the door drew my attention before I could press her on the subject. Jermaine opened the door, finding Barbie outside. She'd opted for black trousers and a white silk sleeve-less top which showed off the toned, sinuous muscle beneath.

Paired with camel shoes and a thin belt in the same tone, she looked like a catwalk model. Again.

Molly was right behind her. 'I brought Molly along,' said Barbie. 'Since we are not going to the banquet, I thought maybe we should all stick together.'

Molly looked a little wobbly I noticed, and her eyes didn't seem to meet in the middle. I snapped my head around to stare at the champagne bucket where I spied the bottle upended in it. Left alone when we went to deal with the body, she'd drunk the lot.

'Are you all right, Molly?' I asked, seeing her sway.

She put a hand out to steady herself against the wall, missed it, and clonked her head on the shade of a lamp. 'I'm a little light-headed,' she admitted. 'This is like the time my boyfriend tried to get me drunk so he could ...'

Unsure what she might be about to reveal, I cut her off quickly. 'Jermaine, perhaps you should take Molly to my bedroom and get her onto the bed. A short nap should help.'

Barbie went to look at the bottle. 'Wow. She drank the value of a house. That's going to be quite the hangover.'

With a nod of my head, I motioned for Barbie to join me in my bedroom. Molly was already on the bed and getting comfortable. It didn't look like she would be awake for very long. Anna and Georgie fussed around my feet so I put them both on the bed where they promptly snuggled up next to the young woman.

Now that we were out of Andrea's earshot, I said, 'We have a lot to do and very little time to do it. It might mean we have to split up. I think Andrea lied about not seeing anyone when she came to the ambassador's door. It might be that she saw the killer.'

'Why would she lie about it?' asked Jermaine.

Feeling my determination rising, I said, 'That's what I intend to find out.' We needed to speak to someone about the call to get a cleaner, I needed to go back to the ambassador's suite and see what the hotel's security team were doing, I needed to check on Wayne, and there were a dozen other tasks already forming a queue behind the most immediate ones.

I was going to have a busy evening, but first on my list was to convinced Andrea to tell me the truth. Coming back out of the bedroom behind Barbie, I called out to her, 'Andrea, we need to discuss why you lied to me about not seeing anyone outside.' I was not of a mind to dither tonight, so I went straight from being nice and supportive to playing hardball.

I got no answer.

'She's gone,' said Barbie, looking around to see if Andrea had simply got up and moved to a different spot in the suite. I checked the bathroom while Jermaine and Barbie looked in the other rooms, then all three of us rushed to the door and went outside.

The hallway was empty.

I cursed myself for being so oblivious. I'd left her unattended and she'd bolted. The moment I asked myself why, fresh clues revealed themselves.

'We have to find her,' I blurted.

Hearing the urgent tone in my voice, Barbie asked, 'What is it, Patty?'

'She said she was a cleaner,' I faced her and Jermaine as I ran a mental checklist. I was leaving my room and might not be back for a while. The dogs were okay. Molly was okay. The question was whether I had everything I needed.

'Yeah, so?' asked Barbie, not following my drift.

'She didn't have any cleaning products with her, and she didn't come with a cleaning cart.'

Barbie's hand went to her mouth. 'She could be the killer.'

I didn't think that would be the case. If she were the killer, she would have done the deed and then quietly escaped. She wouldn't have screamed to get attention. Not unless she were a hired assassin, which might fit, and the person behind the killing wanted the body found at a specific time – like right before the banquet.

Either way, we needed to find her and fast.

'Might she try to escape the hotel, madam?' asked Jermaine, making a great point I hadn't yet considered.

We were already in the hallway, which meant a contingent of the hotel's security were just a few feet away. I rapped my knuckles on the ambassador's door.

A man replied from the other side. 'Who is it?'

'Patricia Fisher. The Maharaja has tasked me with finding out what happened to the ambassador. The policeman in there with you can vouch for me.'

I heard conversation inside though I could not make it out, but whatever they felt they needed to discuss resulted in the door opening a few seconds later. Behind the door was a man in a suit. He had the same sort of edgy, dangerous look about him that I get from Tempest – a fellow private investigator who is ex-military. Tall, lean, and with eyes that seemed to see everything, the man stepped out of my way to let me pass.

He was just one of half a dozen members of the security team in the suite, two of whom were women. They all had the same capable, possible ex-military vibe, and they were led by the woman I met earlier in the reception lobby. I forced my brain to remember her name.

'Lena Glauser, yes?' I approached her with my hand outstretched.

She took it with a firm handshake. 'That's correct.' Her blonde hair was pulled into a tight ponytail that tugged at her face and gave her a huge forehead, I observed, as she stepped forward to meet me. 'You said the Maharaja tasked you with solving the murder?' She sounded dubious about my claim. I had to look up to see her face; she had to be over six feet tall which made her taller than the other woman on her team by half a foot, and she was taller than two of the men.

Dutifully, Jermaine produced one of my business cards, Lena taking it and letting her eyes drop to examine it briefly. 'You work for the Maharaja?' she questioned, still unsure why I might be involved at all.

'Not exactly,' I replied.

Before I could give her an abridged explanation, one of the men stepped up to whisper in her ear. She leaned her head toward him, her eyes flicking to me as he most likely revealed something surprising.

Then nodding she said, 'Yes. I remember now. My apologies, Mrs Fisher. I should have made the connection sooner.' The story of my time in Zangrabar had made world headlines in the summer, so it was no surprise that one or more of them worked out who I was, given the Maharaja's presence tonight. I could see she was tussling with what to say next and guessed correctly that she was going to reject my help. 'I'm afraid the investigation falls under Swiss jurisdiction, Mrs Fisher. I have already spoken with the hotel manager. He will summon special investigators from Bern. They will be here in a few hours.'

'Have you locked down the hotel?' I asked, interrupting her before she could say anything else. 'There was a woman in this room when we discovered the body. She claimed to be a cleaner but had no cleaning products or equipment with her. She came to my suite but vanished just a few moments ago. I believe she knows more than she admits to.'

Just behind Lena, one of the men was talking into a radio, relaying messages to a control room somewhere, I suspected.

'You think her to be the killer?' Lena wanted to know.

I searched my feelings before answering. 'No. I don't think so, but I think she might have seen the killer.'

'What makes you say that?' Lena asked.

'Gut feeling,' I answered honestly. 'She didn't feel like a killer.'

My answer drew a chuckle. Not just from Lena, but her whole team and from Wayne who had remained quiet since we came back into the ambassador's suite. 'I wish I had that kind of magical intuition,' Lena joked with her team. 'That would make our jobs a lot easier.' Turning her attention back to me, she said, 'I'm sorry Mrs Fisher. I'm sure you mean well, and I will not obstruct you if you wish to conduct your own investigation, but I cannot grant you access to the ambassador's room. It will be sealed until the investigators arrive.'

Her attitude annoyed me, but I had no interest in petty competition or ego. I didn't care who caught the killer and revealed the truth, so long as someone did it quickly. However, I doubted Lena Glauser knew how deep the ramifications of the ambassador's death might be. 'Are you aware that this could result in war between two nations and cost many thousands of innocent lives?' Her smile faltered. 'Are you aware that the outcome of this investigation could be on every news channel around the world by tomorrow morning? The ambassador's death may be the catalyst that ruins a peace deal freshly brokered between the two nations. Furthermore, and above all else, we must keep the news of the murder from General

Akbar Armand. He is the ambassador's fellow countryman and representative of Itarnia's armed forces. Are you confident you can solve this case in the next few hours?' Lena was starting to look worried. 'That is all we have. News crews are here tonight. At some point the ambassador's absence will cause suspicion, and by then, we need to have a killer in custody.'

She didn't get to respond because someone started thumping the door. 'Farid,' a man called from outside. 'Farid it is Akbar. Are you unwell? That is what the Maharaja claims.'

'It's the general,' I stated the obvious, putting Lena on the spot. Her eyes went wide with panic, so I did the right thing and stepped in to save her. We were going to have to let the general in and give him reason to think everything was in order. Otherwise his suspicion would deepen, and he might call the hotel's security team to have them open the door. Or maybe he would force his way in since I knew he was here with a contingent of his soldiers.

Going around Lena, I pointed to two of her men. 'Get the ambassador's body. Take it into the bedroom.' They looked at Lena, who nodded her head, seeming glad someone else was in charge. Then I jabbed a finger at Wayne and another of the men. 'Move that rug over the bloodstain.' Looking around quickly and gritting my teeth as my mind raced, I slapped Jermaine on the arm. 'Quick, get that couch and move it onto the rug. That will look more natural.'

'Yes, madam.' He burst into action as I wheeled around to face Barbie.

She sighed and started taking off her clothes. 'Let me guess: I'm a high-class hooker and that is why the ambassador hasn't come down yet. You want me to answer the door in my underwear and tell the general that we haven't finished yet.'

I pulled an apologetic face. 'Sorry, babe. I'd do it, but ...' But I'm in my fifties and my boobs unravel like spaniel's ears now.

Seizing the chance to do something, Lena Glauser said, 'Rosie, you strip too. It will be more believable if there are two of you.'

'What?' Rosie, her junior security guard looked mortified at the idea. She was attractive and had a good body; getting naked wasn't the issue. It was the room full of men she worked with that made her want to keep her clothes on.

The general hammered on the door again. It even sounded like he was using a hammer, the thuds too hard to be made by human flesh. 'Farid.' This time the general sounded concerned.

'Quickly, Rosie,' insisted her boss. 'We don't have time to argue.'

I started moving and raised my hands to either side to move people along. 'Everyone else get into the bedroom.' Poor Rosie had her jacket off and her shirt untucked already, but she wanted the men to leave before anything else came off.

The general hammered and called again. Barbie was ready, wearing a tiny thong and a matching push-up bra, she looked the part so I just had to pray she could pull it off and convince the general to go away.

With a final good luck to both her and Rosie, who was now down to her underwear, I ran for the bedroom.

Barbie shot me a nervous smile and went to the door.

Tucked around the corner of the bedroom door and out of sight with all the others, I could only listen. We all heard the door unlock.

'Who are you?' demanded the general.

'I'm Barbie,' Barbie cooed sexily.

'And I'm Rosie,' said Rosie a moment later. I could imagine them both smiling from the doorway as they did their best to block the general's entry.

'You are white whores,' snapped the general rudely. 'Where is Ambassador Hosseini?'

'He's recovering, sweetie,' cooed Barbie, ignoring the 'whore' comment. 'He said to tell you he'd be along soon. He hasn't finished with us yet.'

The general wasn't going to be dismissed that easily. 'He hired you for sex? Is that what I am supposed to believe?'

Making her voice sound defensive, Barbie said, 'It's a lucrative job, sweetie. I can give you my card if you like.'

'You are lying.' The general sounded utterly certain when he made that statement.

Then we heard the two women cry out. 'Hey!' said Barbie. 'You can't just barge in here!'

I held my breath. The general was inside the suite. How determined would he be? Was he about to search the place? It sounded likely.

'I know you are lying, whore,' spat the general. 'Because the ambassador is a homosexual.'

I closed my eyes and felt like beating my head against a wall. Not that I could have known or had any way by which I could have found out, but it hadn't occurred to me to ever question his sexuality.

'It is why he is here and not in my country where it is still rightfully outlawed. Here among the disgusting infidels, he can do as he pleases,' growled the general, his voice getting louder as he came through the ambassador's suite.

Warning us that he was coming, Barbie shouted, 'Ambassador, sweetie. The general is heading for your bedroom.'

Any second now the man we didn't want to know about the murder was going to come through the bedroom door and there would be no way to prevent him seeing the body: the ambassador was on top of the covers. Had I thought things through a little better, I would have placed him under the covers where we might have been able to say he'd suffered a heart attack or stroke – make his death look like an accident.

I took a deep breath. I was going to whisper instructions to get him into the bed and then go outside to lie through my teeth. I just needed to stall the general for a few seconds. Then, hasty movement behind me, which I had been ignoring, caught me by total surprise as my butler walked by me to get to the door one hundred percent naked.

His muscular buttocks vanished around the doorframe to be greeted by an exclamation from the general. I suspected his outburst would translate to be a number of expletives in Itarnian, but I was still holding my breath as I listened to hear what might happen next.

Any attempt to get the general into the bed now would tip our hand and make the whole ruse appear to be exactly that.

Jermaine's voice echoed back from the suite's main room. 'General, the ambassador respectfully requests that you respect his privacy and leave his accommodation before you see anything else.' His words were delivered with measured dignity and humility.

Unwilling to challenge the naked man and very possibly not wanting to see the scene inside the bedroom, the general accepted Jermaine's words at face value.

He called to the ambassador, 'Farid, you are a disgusting dog. Lying with men and white whores at the same time? Your debauchery knows no bounds! Please do not delay too long. Your host awaits, and his meeting is too important.'

The sound of departing footsteps was accompanied by half a dozen of us finally drawing breath.

When the door closed and the suite was silent again, I heard Barbie say, 'My goodness, Jermaine. Talk about hidden talents.'

I didn't want to see his hidden talent. The sight of his naked bum was already indelibly etched into my brain. I didn't want to see the rest of him.

'Wayne, can you please take him his clothes?' With a chuckle, the agent from Scotland Yard grabbed the discarded bundle of clothes and left the room. The other men went to follow him and found their way blocked by Lena who was giving Rosie and Barbie a minute to get their clothes back on.

Her stern expression stopped the guys from getting an eyeful, though she couldn't resist poking her head out to get a look at Jermaine while pretending to make sure the girls were decent.

We'd averted disaster, or more accurately, Barbie, Rosie, and Jermaine had, but now that people had their clothes back on, and their hidden talents were hidden once more, we still had a crime to solve.

Thief

N ow much more willing to help than she had been five minutes ago, Lena Glauser skipped the part where I felt she ought to apologise, but nevertheless arrived at a place where she felt inclined to offer her help.

She asked, 'What can we do to assist you, Mrs Fisher?'

By now, I'd had long enough for my brain to catch up a little, so Lena got a list. 'I need a list of everyone staying in the hotel. I need to speak to whomever receives the calls for the rooms. According to Andrea ...'

'Wait,' Lena begged. 'Is that the name of the woman who found the body?'

'Yes.'

'Did she show you her identification?'

I shook my head. 'No.'

Barbie came to stand beside me, fiddling with her clothes to get them straight. 'You think she might have given us a false name?'

'It would make sense,' I conceded. 'If she isn't on the level. Anyway,' I returned to the point I had been making, 'according to her, a call came from the ambassador's room requesting some dirty plates be cleaned away. I need to know if there really was a call. If not, it tells us we need to find her because she knows something and might even be the killer. If the call did come in, I want to know what was said.'

Lena snapped out instructions to two of her men who quickly scurried away. 'Anything else?' she asked.

'Yes, do you have pictures of all the staff?'

They did, of course. I could see them all on one of the computers in the hotel's control room located on the ground floor, but when she offered to have a tablet brought up to me, I chose that option instead; I wanted to have a good search of the ambassador's room and belongings.

There is something quite distasteful about going through a dead man's belongings, but I thought it necessary. Wayne was good enough to search his pockets, I really didn't want to do that myself. While Wayne dealt with the icky task, Jermaine, Barbie, and I, started on his drawers, wardrobe, and bags. His bags were empty, the ambassador having efficiently unpacked, but the moment that observation crossed my mind, I instantly questioned it. He was a high-ranking official, a dignitary, and representative of his country. He wouldn't be packing or unpacking his own possessions.

'Where is his assistant?' I asked out loud. All eyes turned to look at me. 'There's no way he was travelling alone.'

Jermaine saw the truth of it instantly. 'He must have at least one member of staff with him.'

I didn't need to prompt Lena to get onto the control hub, she already had her radio in use. A short conversation later, she said, 'The ambassador checked in at two fourteen this afternoon with his aide who registered himself as Behrouz Parastui.'

The sound of fast-approaching footsteps alerted us just before one of her men reappeared. He had the tablet she requested in his hand and I abandoned what I was doing to get a look.

The man must have run most of the way for he was out of breath and beginning to perspire. He handed it over and moved out of the way, his task complete as Lena brought the device to life. He had more to report, though, so after a few seconds to catch his breath he caught Lena's attention.

'Control did not receive a call from this suite at any point today,' he told us calmly. 'I also checked the staff log and there is no one working anywhere in this building with the first name Andrea.'

I cursed my foolishness. Standing by my belief that she wasn't the killer, she was guilty of something and she needed to be found. 'The hotel is sealed, yes?' I confirmed.

Lena said, 'Yes. I have positioned teams at both the main entrance and the staff exit. No one will get out.'

'What about the roof?' I asked.

My question caused a quizzical look from Lena and others. 'You think someone might have a parachute up there?' she asked, a tinkle of amusement in her voice.

'I was thinking more like a paraglider, since you asked.' In my head, I pictured the British secret agent landing on top of the Aurelia as we sailed from Athens.

Lena smiled indulgently. 'Access to the roof is also locked off, Mrs Fisher, you needn't worry. There is an electronic lock that can be activated from the control room. No one, not even a person with a parachute, will escape that way.'

Persisting, I asked 'What if guests go to the front lobby and demand to be released?'

'The team at the exits are armed, Mrs Fisher. They have the only weapons in the building; non-lethal, of course, and they will use them if forced to do so. We do not operate like a hotel because we are not one. The Exclusive is a politically neutral establishment. People who enter the building cross a border and as such we are able to close that border. That is what we have done.'

The information was startling; I hadn't expected it. However, it was also helpful. 'Then we ought to assume she is still inside the building. We need to find her and find out what she knows. In the meantime, I want to know where the Ambassador's assistant is. What room is he staying in?'

Lena dropped her eyes to the tablet where her right hand flittered across the screen. Reading it, her eyes dancing back and forth, she saw something which surprised her. 'I'm not seeing a room assignment.'

I squinted my eyes as I failed to understand what she was telling me. 'He doesn't have a room?'

'No.' Lena was shaking her head; she couldn't understand what she was reading. 'How can there be no room assignment for him?'

'He's staying here, madam,' said Jermaine. When I looked at him, he added, 'He's the ambassador's lover.' Then he stood to one side to show me two different jacket sizes hanging in the wardrobe.

Then, where is he? The question boomed loud in my head. Would he have gone to the banquet ahead of his boss/boyfriend? That sounded unlikely, which meant he was missing, and that didn't bode well.

Barbie raised her hand. The motion caught my eye, but she wasn't raising it like a child in class might to ask permission to speak. She still had her back to everyone as she went through the ambassador's drawers and her hand was up to get our attention.

When we fell silent, she slowly turned about to look at me, chewing her bottom lip a little as if caught in indecision. 'I think he might have been robbed.'

Her comment made my eyebrows jump and now she had our attention, she stepped back so we could gather around and look into the top drawer. 'This looks like a man's jewellery box to me,' she said. 'But there's nothing in it. Why would he bring it if it is empty?'

'He wouldn't,' said Jermaine. 'I think you might be right.'

Lena looked at the box. No one touched it because there might be fingerprints. She tutted. Then she revealed something I'm sure she didn't want to. 'This probably is a theft. We've had several over the last few months and haven't been able to catch the person doing it or work out how they are getting the items from the building. Mr Hingis – that's the hotel manager – refuses to believe there even is a thief. He thinks the metal detectors at the exits make it impossible for anyone to take items of value out and since all the reported thefts were of jewellery, the metal detector would find them. The thief never leaves a trace, certainly not a fingerprint, and I'm sure this will be the same. I'll have it scanned, but I'm not hopeful.'

The box was large enough to hold several items of men's jewellery: watches, cufflinks, maybe even some rings. That it was completely empty suggested a thief had been in the room. Was that Andrea? If so, did she also kill the ambassador? Did he surprise her?

I went outside to the main part of the suite. As I left the ambassador's bedroom, the spot on the floor where the ambassador had been was right in front of me.

'What is it, Patty?' asked Barbie as she watched me tilt my head. I held a finger up to beg a moment's grace because I had just spotted something. I walked across to the desk to look at the envelopes there. I tilted my head left and right and skewed my lips as I stared. Someone, the ambassador or his aide, had been going through them but had been stopped halfway through the task because half were opened, and half were not. I looked at them, but none were in English and it probably meant nothing, so I went back to what I had been doing and walked to the front door. It was down a short hallway, so when I turned around and looked, the spot where we found the ambassador's body was no longer in sight.

'She didn't see it on the way in,' I announced mostly to myself. Nodding that I had it right, I walked the path I would take if I were a thief heading for the bedroom. Andrea, or whatever her real name was, would have exited the hallway and turned right. She would have to look left to see the body. Barbie continued to watch me and had been joined by Lena and the others as everyone now came to see what I was doing.

Looking them in the eye, I said, 'She must have knocked, confirmed there was no one here and then gone straight for the bedroom. She only saw the body on her way out which was when she screamed.' Letting my shoulders slump for a second as the mystery got even deeper and the challenge we faced got yet harder, I blew out a hard breath to shake the feeling of hopelessness and told myself to rally. 'We need to find Andrea. I think we can assume that's not her real name. She might not even work here, but we should go through all the staff pictures and be sure.'

'I'll do that,' volunteered Jermaine.

'We can do that with this tablet,' said Lena, holding the device up. 'We might be better moving to the control room though.' She looked at me. 'You said you wanted a list of everyone staying here? Well, I can have that list printed off, but I think we can put faces to most of the people if we go back through the lobby footage - there are cameras there. I've never had to do it before, but apart from when people arrive as a gaggle, we should be able to use the check-in time to identify them.'

That sounded good. I needed to find a corner of this mystery to pick at. So far, I was getting nowhere, and the pesky clock continued to tick. A theft, a murder, a missing person. What might be next?

Control Room

W e made the decision to all go. 'I want to see the staff pictures too,' I announced. 'And I want to see if we can identify the ambassador's assistant on the camera. I want to know what he looks like.'

I wanted Barbie and Jermaine with me; it just felt safer for all of us if we stuck together. It certainly felt safer for me if I had Jermaine close. The mostly silent Wayne Garrett came too. Like an extra shadow, he refused to let me be out of his sight for more than a few moments. He'd relaxed when we first arrived at the hotel, believing, he said, that it was a safe environment where the Godmother couldn't stage an attack. He no longer felt as certain. Or he felt that maybe there was a fresh threat.

Before heading downstairs, I went to my room to check on Molly. I found her beneath the covers of my bed which meant she was alert enough to decide she would be more comfortable there. Her shoes were on the floor where she'd kicked them off. Anna and Georgie came to the edge of the bed with their tails wagging.

Mother and daughter wanted to come with me. Or maybe they just wanted some exercise, but I didn't want to leave them cooped up, so I plopped them on the floor and asked Jermaine to find their leads and collars.

This was so far from the evening I'd planned that it was unrecognisable. A frustrated sigh escaped my lips as we walked along the hallway to find the elevators. 'How're you doing, Patty?' Barbie asked, nudging my arm with her elbow in a playful way. 'Isn't that nice David Sebastian supposed to be here tonight? Were you hoping to see him?'

I snorted at the mention of his name because I'd forgotten all about him. I had enough man worries with my impending divorce without adding new ones, and I was about to go back to the Aurelia where I would have to make a decision about my feelings for the captain, Alistair Huntley.

I really didn't want to discuss any of it right now, not least because it would feel self-indulgent to chat about my man worries in the middle of a murder investigation, but mostly because I had no idea how I ought to feel. To dodge the subject, I asked her, 'What was the general like? Was he old? Did he ogle you?'

Barbie shuddered at the memory. 'Actually, he was fine. Yes, he's old. Late fifties I would guess, so not exactly old, but not young either. He's handsome, truth be told, tall and athletic with good hair and a strong chin. It was his assistant that gave me the creeps.'

Just behind us, Rosie spoke up. 'Yeah, he was creepy. He wouldn't stop looking at my boobs.'

Barbie swung her head around to look at her. 'I know, right. He was just a bit too pervy and he had this false hand.'

'False hand?' I questioned.

Barbie nodded. 'His left hand is missing. He had a prosthetic hand but not a modern one that you could pick things up with, it looked like a big rubber or plastic thing and it made his arm look too long.'

'And he had a missing eye,' chipped in Rosie. 'He must have been in an accident at some point because his head had scars all over it.'

'You think he was the general's assistant?' I asked, wondering who the other man might be.

'Aide-de-camp,' said Rosie.

She got a, 'Huh?' from me and Barbie and everyone else.

'That's the name for a general's assistant. I used to be in the army,' she explained. 'It won't be hard to find out who he is. He'll be on the guest list.'

Remembering the hammering sound when the general wanted to get into the ambassador's room, I connected it to the aide-de-camp's fake hand. It made sense that the general wouldn't knock when he had a person to do that for him.

Talk of the injured man drove away my thoughts of the men in my life, but wouldn't you know it? The elevator doors opened and there was David Sebastian waiting to get out.

'Patricia!' he beamed like we were long lost friends. 'I was worried when you didn't show at the banquet. I had to bribe a member of staff to tell me which room you are in.'

'Oh, really?' said Lena, taking interest instantly. 'Which member of staff was it, please?'

David was standing inside the elevator but wasn't getting out as it was clear we were all looking to get in. He backed away to give us room as the dachshunds tried to climb his legs.

Distracting him so he couldn't answer Lena's question, I moved him into the corner of the steel box as the door swished closed. 'David, I don't have time to attend the banquet. I have ... I have become caught up in something that happened earlier this evening. I expect to be busy for the rest of the night.'

He nodded along as I spoke, hanging off my words and as I thought about what to say next, I couldn't help but notice how handsome he looked in his dinner jacket and bow tie. He had a trace of tan to his face which gave him a healthy, vibrant glow. I had no doubt it was deliberate; he spent a lot of his time being photographed and attending public events. Lost in my own thoughts, I missed what he said and had to ask him to repeat himself.

'I asked if it was to do with the soldiers getting antsy downstairs?' he said for the second time. In the tight confines of the elevator car, he had everyone's attention. What had we missed?

'Whose soldiers?' I asked.

With an expression that underlined the concern I felt, he said, 'All of them. The Maharaja is able to remain above it all, but it is clear there is some tension between General Armand and his honour guard and the Maharaja's Royal Guard.'

'How bad is it?' I begged to know.

He wriggled his lips as he looked for the right words, settling on, 'Let's just say it's a good thing no one is armed tonight.' He pulled a face of concern. 'General Armand seemed to be the problem. That was my take anyway. Bertie, the foreign minister,' he supplied in case I didn't know who Bertie was, 'he thinks the situation is more precarious than anyone knows. If something happens tonight, the hostilities between their countries could resume but on a worse scale than before. The ambassador needs to get to the banquet and calm things down before they escalate.'

'That's not going to happen,' I said before I thought to still my tongue.

David was bright enough that he made the jump instantly. 'Is that what you are up to, Patricia? That's why you are not at the banquet?' He put a grateful hand to his chest. 'I thought maybe you were avoiding me. Has something happened to the ambassador?'

Now I was stuck. I didn't want to lie to him; there were enough people telling lies already, but the lift pinged to announce its arrival on the ground floor. 'I have to go, David,' I told him as I moved to the doors.

'I'm coming with you, Patricia. I'd rather that than return to the international incident waiting to happen upstairs.'

I could have convinced him to leave me if I'd wanted to. Or I could have asked Lena to deny him entry to the control room, but I did neither. He was sweet for me and he was sweet himself and I constantly felt like I was pushing him away without reason to do so.

Instead, I said nothing and let him join in. It was quite the team I'd managed to assemble already.

In the control room, heads turned as we came in. Seeing them, Anna gave an experimental wag of her tail; a sign that she felt unsure about the situation she now found herself in. Were the humans here friendly?

There were two walls of tv monitors showing different parts of the hotel. It wasn't the inside of guests' rooms, obviously, which was a pity because we could solve the crime right now if they recorded the murder, but it did show the front lobby where I could now see three security guards. Most of the other cameras showed the carpark, the street outside and some of the central areas.

A tall, thin man came toward us. His scalp was devoid of hair; he didn't even have eyebrows I noticed as he approached. 'What's going on, Lena?' he asked, his eyes on me and my friends and not on her as he posed the question. 'Who are these people? And why do they have dogs with them.' Anna strained forward to sniff his leg and I missed the early days when I first got her, and she would have attacked his ankle.

Lena stepped around me to block his path. 'Mr Hingis, this is the team appointed by the Maharaja to investigate the ambassador's murder. They have been most helpful already. I think we should assist them, sir.'

I thrust out my hand and gave him a friendly smile. 'Hello, I'm Patricia.'

Mr Hingis, the hotel manager, took my hand. It was a bit like shaking hands with a dead fish. He looked at me and then at my friends, but when he spoke, it was to his head of security. 'Glauser we have special investigators coming from Switzerland. I thought I made it clear that the deceased's room was to be sealed and left for them.'

'The situation is not as we originally thought, sir. There have been developments,' Lena tried to explain but he cut her off.

'I am not interested in developments, Glauser. When I give instructions, I expect them to be followed.'

Beginning to find myself irritated, I got involved. 'Have you any idea what is happening here tonight?' I snapped at him. 'The ambassador's death could be the spark that ignites a war. It is imperative that the killer be identified as swiftly as possible, and certainly before the rest of the Itarnian party find out.'

The hotel manager's eyes flared wide as he shot a look at Lena. 'I ordered you to inform the Itarnian party!'

My irritation was about to shift into high gear. 'Are you completely stupid?' He snapped his face back to mine and tried unsuccessfully to stare me down. 'If General Armand finds out his ambassador is dead, he will go berserk and ruin the peace the two countries have just achieved. Whoever is responsible for the murder most likely perpetrated the act with the specific aim of restarting the war. You must give us time to investigate. If we inform the Itarnians their ambassador is dead and cannot tell them who the killer is, they will assume it is one of the Zangrabarians. You'll have a battle inside the hotel.'

'We are prepared for a battle, woman.' That he refused to use my name was equivalent to an open-handed slap. 'But since they have no weapons, I doubt much will happen. I have no interest in their politics or problems. My job is to do what is right, and in this case the right thing is to inform the Itarnians that a member of their delegation has been killed.'

Arguing any further was senseless, but he chose to leave before I could reply. 'I want them out of here, Glauser. They have no right to be in my control room. Send them back to the party and tell the Itarnians their ambassador is dead. If I have to tell you again, it will not go well for you. Is that clear?'

'Crystal clear, sir,' Lena snapped out her reply smartly.

I felt he was clear too. As hotel manager it ought to be his job to deliver the news. He looked to be shirking his responsibility and while he could be the one to eject us from the room, he didn't want to be involved. I'd met people like him before: content to give orders, but they don't actually want to do anything.

He left through a door without glancing back once, and once it closed, I felt the whole room breathe a sigh of relief. A few feet away, Lena muttered some obscenities specifically aimed at her boss. She was justified to do so; the man is an arrogant, ignorant arse, but I had no time for such indulgences. Dismissing him just as swiftly as he had us, I asked Lena, 'Where can we review the footage to find the ambassador's aide?'

'I have that right here,' called a young woman with her hand up. She was positioned in front of a bank of monitors with her back to us. I started in her direction.

'You also want to review staff pictures,' Lena reminded me.

'I'll attend to that, madam,' said Jermaine.

Hoping he would be able to spot Andrea, I focussed my attention on finding the Ambassador. David tapped my arm to get my attention. 'I can't believe Ambassador Hosseini is dead!' he hissed. 'I almost choked when Glauser said it. Now you're investigating what happened to him? I suppose that's why you weren't at the banquet.'

'The Maharaja hopes I can find the killer quickly. He plans to tell General Armand himself once he can give him the full story of what happened.'

David asked, 'But what if the killer is from Zangrabar? What if it's one of the Maharaja's soldiers?'

'Then the Maharaja will have a problem still and a tough decision to make.' It could easily be one of his own men, or someone else from Zangrabar. I hadn't made it to the banquet and was yet to get my hands on a guest list, but I was willing to bet the Itarnians were only a fraction of the people attending. There were British politicians here, my party of friends, and undoubtedly some other people, but the bulk of the gathering was successful Zangrabar nationals living and working in England plus staff from the Zangrabar embassy.

I got to the woman with her hand up. David and Barbie were with me. 'Hi, I'm Patricia. What've you got?'

'I'm Chantelle,' the woman replied, smiling at Anna and Georgie before reaching out to point at a screen with her right arm. 'That's the ambassador right there. That was at 1414hrs when he arrived.' She advanced the screen a few frames. 'Is this the gentlemen you are looking for? He signed in as Behrouz Parastui. He and the ambassador were assigned to the same suite.'

'Then I guess that's him. But where is he?' I murmured to myself. The man was at least twenty years younger than the ambassador; somewhere in his early thirties would be my guess though it was hard to be sure looking at him on a screen. We had a face, and that was a start, but now we had to find him.

'Most of the guests are in the banquet room,' Chantelle told us.

'Who is he?' asked David. 'The ambassador's aide?'

'And lover, it would seem.' I looked around to see how Jermaine was getting on. Sitting in a chair while the security team member, who had just vacated it, helped him to use the system, he navigated through staff pictures. They had a head shot for everyone, but it looked like he had to go through them one at a time.

Just then, Andrea's face appeared on the screen and he twitched in his seat. 'That's her,' he claimed triumphantly.

Lena and other members of her team came to look. 'That's Martha Grimes.' Lena looked confused. 'This is the woman you discovered in the ambassador's room?'

'Yes,' replied Jermaine. 'She told us she was sent there to collect some dirty plates.'

Lena spun around to face her team. 'Has anyone seen her today?' When no one admitted having done so, she crossed the room to a computer and slid in front of it. She was muttering a running commentary as she tapped at the keyboard. 'I don't even think she's working today, but even if she were, there would be no reason for her to be in anyone's room; she's a chef.'

'What's going on?' demanded Hingis. He'd re-entered the room when none of us were looking. 'Why are these people still here? Have you informed the Itarnians about the ambassador's death yet?'

'I think we may have found our thief, sir,' Lena replied, her eyes still on the computer screen.

Drearily, he snapped at her, 'What has that got to do with any of the orders I gave you?'

'She was in the ambassador's room, sir. She could be the killer, but she is definitely the thief and she emptied the ambassador's room of jewellery.'

'I don't care!' Hingis shouted, spittle flying from his lips as he raged.

'I say,' said David. 'Steady on now. Your people are just trying to do their jobs.'

The hotel manager rounded on him instantly. 'Their jobs are to do what I say, not chase glory by trying to find a murderer.'

With patient calm, Lena pointed to Martha's picture on the computer screen. 'But you were shouting at me just last week for even suggesting there is a thief. Now we've identified who it is.'

Hingis looked at the photograph and pursed his lips. 'Where is your evidence?'

'Martha Grimes is one of our chefs. There was an incident a year ago when a wallet went missing. She was suspected, but nothing could be proven. I always thought she was guilty. Do you remember that, sir? I wanted to go after her, but you made me fill in paperwork and had her sign it to say that she gave permission to have her locker searched.'

'Yes, I remember,' he sneered. 'You were wrong., There was nothing in her locker.'

'That's because you made me fill out your stupid paperwork. It gave her all the time she needed to hide the wallet somewhere else. How will it look when the killer turns out to be a member of the Exclusive's staff?'

Hingis scoffed, 'There is no thief, Glauser. You think a chef, or anyone for that matter, could manage to leave the premises with stolen goods? Everyone passes through a metal detector on their way in and again on their way out. With my policies in place it is impossible to steal jewellery.' He shared his smile with the room; Glauser's theories were a big joke.

'Why would she be on the guest floors dressed in a staff uniform when she has only ever been issued chef's whites, sir? There are items missing from the ambassador's room, she had no right or reason to be anywhere near it, she gave a false name, scarpered before the security team arrived and is definitely here today without booking in. How would you explain it, sir?' She'd pinned him with his own stupidity and everyone in the room knew it. Going for the kill wasn't a wise move in so public a forum, but she'd obviously suffered him for long enough because that's what she did. 'What do you feel my next move should be, sir? Shall I dispatch the security team to search the hotel high and low until we find her? Or shall I take a leaf from your book and sit on my arse?'

Hingis went purple. 'You can consider yourself suspended, Glauser,' he spat.

She threw her radio to Rosie, who caught it, dropped it, juggled it, and finally clutched it to her chest. 'No need. I quit. You're an idiot, and I'll not work with you any longer.'

'For me, Glauser!' he shouted as she went for the door. 'You work for me, not with me!'

As she spun about and left the room, I wondered what might happen now. She had been my ally and I wasn't going to get any help from Hingis.

Embarrassed silence stretched on for too many seconds as no one dared to speak. I used the time to ask myself what else I needed to find out while I was in the control room.

A bark from Hingis broke my concentration. 'Get back to work all of you or there'll be more jobs lost tonight.' His staff, fearful enough that he might mean what he said, made themselves look busy. Rosie rushed out the same door Lena left through, dropping the extra radio onto a counter as she went.

Unwilling to beat around the bush, I met Hingis head on. 'Mr Hingis, the Maharaja of Zangrabar needs your help, sir. Will you go beyond the remit of your job and help us avert a war? I need to find Martha Grimes and Behrouz Parastui. They are both in this hotel somewhere.'

He wheeled around to look me in the eye and I already knew his answer before he spoke. With two fingers, he summoned a pair of men dressed in the security team uniform. 'Elgin. Danuser. Escort these civilians from my control room, please.'

He expected me to meekly leave, which is why I didn't. His nostrils flared as I stepped into his personal space and looked right up at them. 'Lena was right, you are an idiot. You're so busy attempting to fortify the crumbling foundations on which your powerbase is built, that you not only turned down help from an Agent of Scotland Yard,' Wayne waved his hand, 'but you chose to insult the Maharaja's personal guests.' Panic hit his eyes. 'What do you think your most honoured guest will have to say to your boss about that?'

'I ...'

The moment he spoke, I broke eye contact and started toward the door. Barbie, Jermaine, David, and Wayne moved with me.

'Ma'am, I, ah. That is to say ...' Hingis was hurrying after me, his haughtiness abandoned as he stared a stern reprimand, demotion, or perhaps dismissal in the face. He couldn't find it in himself to apologise though and got no chance because Jermaine stepped in when he tried to reach for my arm.

I think he intended to stop my exit and beg my forgiveness. But his hand was caught by my butler's lightning-fast reflexes. 'Step back now, sir,' he chided.

I glanced across at Chantelle, who was unable to hide her smirk.

Feeling good about humiliating the man was petty, but I did it anyway.

Outside the door to the control room, we found someone was waiting for us.

Going to the Banquet

'He's not bright enough to make sure I leave the building,' said Lena with a chuckle as her two male former subordinates did exactly as Hingis said by leaving us outside the control room. 'It's a shame because I liked this job. I just couldn't deal with him. I should have kept hold of my radio though; that would help immensely.'

'This radio?' asked Wayne, producing his right hand from behind his back. He'd swiped it on his way out. 'I thought it might come in handy too. I was just going to listen on it, but maybe you can rally the troops to your cause. I don't think many of them are on his side.'

'None of us are on his side,' said Rosie, slipping through the door to join us in the hallway.

Lena shook her head. 'Rosie you should head back in before he catches you. He'll get replaced soon enough. You can put up with him for a little longer.'

'I think I'll take my chances, thank you.' Rosie sounded determined. 'Besides, there's a lot of hotel to search and you need all the help you can get.'

'Where do we start?' asked Barbie.

I checked my watch. 'Lena, will the security team still do as you ask?'

It was Rosie who answered. 'Yes, they will. Hingis has no idea what half of us do anyway.'

I nodded slowly, thoughts cascading through my brain. Then I took David's hand, much to his surprise. 'Lord mayor, I think you should take me to the banquet.'

We left Lena and Rosie to coordinate those team members they thought they could rely on and went back to our suites. It was quick-change time. If we were to move among the guests at the banquet, we would need to look like them, so the expensive-as-unicorn's-horn dress came out of its wrapper once more and this time I put it on. David waited in my suite's central area with a gin and tonic Jermaine fixed him. There was one for me too, which I downed in two hits once dressed again. Jermaine zipped me up and checked in on Molly.

She was snoring like a warthog, flat on her back with her mouth wide open. It was loud enough that even the dogs shied away, Anna jumping onto the couch where she curled into a ball and closed her eyes. Poor Georgie didn't have the height or perhaps strength to follow her mother, so I found her dancing on her back legs and yipping for assistance.

I tucked her up next to her mother and went to find Barbie. Jermaine had never changed out of his dinner jacket, but now Wayne had also donned his. The three men's outfits were now the same in all but shoe style.

We found Barbie outside closing the door to her room, and moments later we were heading back down in the elevator yet again. I wanted to speak with the Maharaja; to give him an update, but I also wondered if I might find Andrea/Martha or even Behrouz Parastui among the guests. Their whereabouts were unknown but that didn't mean they weren't in the banquet room. Behrouz could be unaware of the ambassador's death and Martha might be trying to steal purses for all I knew.

It was worth a shot and I wanted to know more about the political end of this drama, for which I was going to leverage David's friendship with the British Foreign Minister. He would be able to explain the relationships and point out General Armand.

Why did I want to know all that? Taking a breath in the control room, right before Hingis threw us out, I did what I should have done right at the start and asked myself my favourite question: who stands to gain?

The most obvious answer came back to the likely ramifications of the ambassador's death. An Itarnian dignitary murdered brutally while at a party thrown by the ruler of long-time enemy, Zangrabar. Blame Zangrabar and restart the war. The one person who came out on top in that situation was the general commanding the Itarnian armed forces. It was suggested right at the start of course, though I chose to ignore opinion so it wouldn't cloud my judgement. There was just one problem with making the ambassador's murder the work of General Armand: it had a major flaw. Why didn't he insist on seeing the ambassador when he came to his suite? If he was guilty of arranging the man's death to further his own cause, and this was his moment to reveal it, then why didn't he? Instead, he acted as if he believed the ambassador was in his bedroom and allowed Jermaine's hidden talent to scare him away.

It followed though, that if the Itarnian general could be guilty, then so too could be any of his soldiers or even a member of the Zangrabar forces. Who did the Maharaja have with him? Either side would have people, civilian and military, who might loathe the concept of a brokered peace. Neither side had won so one might argue that all the blood and tears of the past were for naught. I knew so little about the region, and cursed myself for that lack of knowledge, but as the elevators opened, the delightful sounds of live music reached our ears, I knew I could take nothing for granted, not even the word of the Maharaja.

Not until I knew the truth.

David offered me his elbow, a happy smile on his face as I looped my arm through it. He was a gentleman at all times and very easy to like. However, I wasn't letting my mind be distracted by any stray thoughts as my eyes roved the room. Every face got a second of inspection before I moved on. The missing man and woman were somewhere inside this hotel.

They could be anywhere, but currently, they were the only leads I had to pursue.

David attempted to steer me in a direction I wasn't ready to go. 'You want to meet the foreign minister, yes?' he asked when I resisted.

'Not yet.' I'd just spotted General Armand and I wanted to spend a moment watching him.

The banquet room was a triple height ornate room where the walls were inlaid with gold and the floors, pillars and doorframes were hewn from marble. A high table set on a platform a foot above the rest of the floor held the Maharaja and his most important guests. I would have been at a table nearby but two seats along from the Maharaja was General Armand and to the general's left sat his aide-de-camp who I could recognise from Rosie's description. I had to feel sorry for the poor man, for his face was ruined.

Between the general and the Maharaja was an empty seat, the one which should be filled by the ambassador; I found the void hard to look at. To the right of the Maharaja was another soldier, the head of Zangrabar's armed forces I assumed. The Maharaja mentioned him earlier and his desire to have the two opposing generals seen eating together.

I wasn't sure if that was going to work because the ice between the two nations was palpable even from across the room.

I continued scanning faces until Barbie reappeared. 'I've drawn a blank,' she admitted. So too Jermaine a few moments later when he returned from his roving tour of the room.

It had been a long shot, so I had to pray that Lena and her team would fare better searching the rest of the hotel.

I gave David's arm a squeeze. 'Take me to see your friend, please, but let's keep the ambassador's death on the quiet.'

Foreign Policy

'**G**ood lord, David, where did you get to? You've been gone an age.' I recognised the British Foreign Minister from appearances on the news or in the newspaper. He was a politician from the Conservative Party called Timothy Smith, a name which was common enough to get him the support of the people. I didn't know anything else about him other than he was friends with the Lord Mayor of Kent. He looked from David to me, his eyes taking in my appearance without being lecherous. 'Goodness, is this your date for the night? I say, old boy, well done.' He got to his feet so he could meet me properly.

David rolled his eyes. 'Timothy, this is Patricia Fisher.'

'Timothy Smith at your service, m' lady.' He bowed his head. 'Of course, I already know who you are, Patricia. I do try to keep up with current affairs so I heard all about your exploits in Zangrabar and other places. Jolly well done, that's what

I say.' Then he leaned to one side to look around David at Barbie. 'I see you brought a friend for me?' he said hopefully.

Barbie giggled, which was the most polite thing she could do for him since he looked genuinely hopeful.

Steering him back to the matter at hand, I said, 'I hoped to pick your brain about the tension between the two nations and who might benefit most from the current peace treaty failing.'

'Really?' the foreign minister said while retaking his seat. 'Goodness, well it's fascinating stuff but no one ever wants me to talk about it. I dare say most people find it boring. How in depth do you want me to go?'

I sucked in a deep breath. 'How much can you squeeze into ten minutes?' We were still running against the clock.

Settled in our chairs, David poured me a glass of water from a fresh pitcher on the table. I thanked him and sipped at it as Timothy started talking.

'Firstly, I need to go back in time just a little. Back to the second world war. The British Empire still stretched around the globe back then. Many of the countries we controlled then have since been granted independence. Itarnia is one of those nations, but we were the dominant force in the region, with control over most countries and influence in others. Had our governments been less circumspect, we might have retained control of the region, but it was considered at the time that the locals would be best off running their own business. It was a scrappy land where no established borders existed, and each country had different opinions about where their land ended, and their neighbour's began.'

'Hence the dispute between Itarnia and Zangrabar,' I guessed.

'Exactly, my dear, exactly. Unfortunately, the British thought they were clever enough to solve all the problems by drawing defined borders. We marked them on a map and had the ruling families agree to them. Of course, we were the ones elevating the families to ruling status, so they would agree to anything we said.'

'But the rest of the nation disagreed and that caused fighting over who owned the borders?'

'Yes. For some this happened straight away but only on a small scale. Imagine if you were Scottish and had been proudly Scottish for generations and then someone redraws the border and tells you that you are now English.'

His example drove the concept home nicely. The Scottish people don't want to go to war with England, but they have in the past and for good reason: we were never a good neighbour. We were a bully, and even today, the Scottish cheer for whoever our sporting teams are playing against as a demonstration of how much they don't like us.

Timothy continued to explain the region's history. 'British garrisons put the fighting down by force, which masked the issue rather than deal with it. Decades later, with vastly superior weapons, oil is found in the region and suddenly the land, which has been disputed for a generation, is now potentially worth billions and becomes a matter of national imperative.'

'The piece of land Itarnia and Zangrabar are fighting over is just like that, isn't it?'

The foreign minister nodded glumly. 'Yes. This really is an example of the sins of the father coming back to bite the son. We did this to ourselves. Only, the British left the region decades ago, so really, we did it to them. That's why I have been so involved in trying to undo it. They have a brokered peace, the young Maharaja is quite the politician, but I cannot be certain it will last.'

'Why is that?' I asked.

'Too much bad blood. Too many years of lives lost bickering over something that might be nothing more than desert with no worth at all.'

'Is that likely?' asked Barbie, chipping in a question for the first time. 'I had a boyfriend once who worked in the oil industry. He said finding oil is easy now with modern technology. Surely they can tell if there is mineral wealth beneath the sand?'

Timothy smiled broadly and nodded his head. 'Brains as well as beauty, my dear? Are you perhaps single and looking for a boring older man to keep you?' Barbie giggled at him while David rolled his eyes. I wasn't sure the foreign minister was joking. Moving on before he embarrassed himself, he said, 'You're right, of course. Both sides deny it, but they know as well as we do that there are billions of barrels of oil beneath the desert that divides them. That they have agreed to mine it together and split the wealth may seem friendly and cooperative but may yet lead to war. Their relationship teeters on a knife edge.'

I asked the direct question. 'Do you think something as simple as a death here tonight could pitch the two sides against one another again?'

He gasped in horror. 'Oh, goodness me, yes. It wouldn't take much to set General Armand off. He was dead set against relinquishing the areas his forces had control of and he has a lot of support back home. He's been the leader of their armed forces for almost twenty years. Itarnia has been through four prime ministers in the same period. His face is the one the nation knows.'

The Maharaja said earlier that he could stage a coup and probably win.

A commotion across the room reached a level of noise that no one could ignore. What the foreign minister had to tell me was fascinating, but I lost track of what he was saying when the shouting started.

Looking up, I saw General Armand and his aide get to their feet. I didn't hear what he said, but given the spittle flying from his lips and the accusing finger being jabbed in the direction of the Maharaja, I had to guess he'd been informed of the ambassador's demise.

I was instantly on my feet.

'What's going on?' asked David, rising too and peering across the room.

I didn't have time or need to answer, but heading for the top table, I murmured, 'I think all hell's about to break loose.'

I had to weave through guests and staff alike to cross the room, Wayne, Jermaine, and Barbie right behind me. As we neared the table, so too did the hotel's security, half a dozen of them in suits moving in to prevent bloodshed.

Now close enough, I could hear what was being said. 'This is on you! Did he stumble across your plot?' raged General Armand. 'This is your doing. You arranged this event. Did you do this just so you could take me out? Huh? Lure the head of Itarnia's forces here and kill him so you can attack with our forces in disarray? I warned the prime minister this would be your ploy. Are your forces already poised to invade?' he spoke calmly but through gritted teeth and I could see a vein throbbing at the side of his head. General Armand's aide stood by his shoulder, backing him all the way.

The war looked to be about to start at the banquet.

The Zangrabarian general, who I now knew to be called Farhoud was incensed by the accusation levied at his king. 'How dare you, Armand?'

The Maharaja was swift to quieten his highest-ranking soldier. 'General Farhoud, please,' he begged in a tone that insisted on compliance. Then the young leader turned toward his aggressor. 'General Armand, my nation and I want nothing but peace. The senseless killing over ground which may or may not contain oil is unnecessary. Your prime minister and I agreed to mine the land together, both nations sharing the cost and any profit. You were there for the negotiations, General.' He took a moment and made a show of having nothing in his hands. 'There is no hostility here, General. Your missing guard has not been murdered by my men because he uncovered a plot to kill you here.'

Missing guard? So, it wasn't the ambassador General Armand was getting so excited about. One of his men had absconded.

'That is what you must say until you are ready to spring your trap, Maharaja,' General Armand glowered back at him. 'If you plan to use me as a pawn in this game, you shall have no luck. Hold me hostage here and I will gladly die for the security of my nation.'

The Maharaja pursed his lips and bowed his head. He was losing already, and the ambassador's death was yet to be revealed. This was supposed to be a peaceful photo opportunity but was becoming anything but.

When he looked back up there was steel in the young king's eyes. 'General, I will not allow you to deliberately scupper the peace your nation and mine have finally secured. I will provide you with every resource I have at hand to locate your missing man. I only ask that when he is located, you will return to my table and dine with me. Our differences have been placed in the past and that is where they must stay. I beg that you help me forge a new future for our nations for the prosperity and wellbeing of all our citizens.'

General Armand continued to glare down at the smaller man, but he had no reply. Both sides were surrounded by a contingent of the hotel's security who looked bewildered as to how they should proceed. Hingis was nowhere in sight, but the general turned smartly about and strode away, dragging his aide and anyone else in Itarnian uniform with him.

As they departed, I heard the aide-de-camp shout, 'Scour the hotel. Find him.'

The room was near deathly silent, all eyes on the top table where the Maharaja now stood with his own general. Most people were gawping and unsure what they ought to now do. Many might decide it was time to leave but they didn't yet know the hotel had been sealed to deny the killer the chance to escape.

By my ear, Barbie whispered, 'What if the general's man is dead?'

I didn't get a chance to answer because Rosie appeared. 'Mrs Fisher,' she spoke quietly so only the immediate group would be able to hear. 'We've found something. Can you come with me?'

Booty

T he something they found was a key inside Martha's locker. Martha was still to be located but they'd gone straight to her personal possessions. Her locker contained very little of interest: three sets of chef's whites, a bag of makeup presumably for when she left work each day, a half empty pack of tampons, a few other items, and a key. The key was in the back corner of the locker inside the pouch of an old ratty notebook a person would never look twice at. Upon finding the shiny new key in such an obscure place, they questioned whether it had been there for years, forgotten or lost, or if it was there deliberately because Martha wanted no one to find it.

One of the maintenance chaps told them that type of dimple key was only used on four locks in the entire building. He couldn't identify which one it might open just by looking at it, but it took them less than five minutes to find the lock it opened.

Rosie led us to the ground floor and a maintenance area intended for staff only. The walls were breeze block and unpainted in stark contrast to the gold and marble everywhere else. Through a door with a slotted keyhole, we found Lena and three other members of the security team plus a man in workman's clothes - the maintenance chap, no doubt. As I looked at him, I noticed that he was staring open-mouthed at Barbie. Well, he wasn't the first. I had to guess the security guards were Lena's defectors; those who would rather lose their jobs than work under Hingis any longer. Or maybe they were hedging their bets that they could save the day and, in the aftermath, get Lena reinstated and Hingis fired.

Either way, they moved apart as we approached to show me what they had found.

'This is the outer wall to the building,' Lena explained.

We were looking at the white, plastic cover of an electrical panel of breaker switches. The outer cover was clear plastic to show the row of switches inside. Clearly, I was supposed to see something but though I stared at it, I failed to see the incongruity.

'That's clever,' said Barbie.

Wayne snorted a chuckle. 'It's so good it's all but invisible.'

'That's why I didn't see it,' whined the man in workman's clothes.

'No one is blaming you,' Lena assured him.

I still couldn't see what they were seeing. 'What?' I asked. If it were not an electrical panel, I might have ventured to poke at it, but I didn't trust electricity and preferred to keep my distance.

Jermaine pointed: everyone could see it but me. 'Madam, there are no cables going into the panel.'

I stared at it in disbelief. How had I not noticed that?

Now that we understood we were looking at a fake panel, Lena nodded to Marco. He stepped forward, grasped the panel, and with a click, it swung outward. Behind the false panel, several bricks had been carefully removed to make a hole through to the outside of the building where I could see the white plastic of another false cover. Inside the hole was a small, black velvet bag and inside that I knew we were going to find the ambassador's jewellery.

Lena stepped up to the panel and took the bag. 'The panel on the other side opens on the street. It's just above head height so very few people would ever look at it and it is in a blind spot where none of our cameras ever sweep. Outside it is just a flat plastic panel. I think she's been stealing from the hotel guests since we took her on more than a year ago. She didn't need to defeat the metal detector because she went around it. It would have taken her a while to whittle out the mortar between the bricks, but I have to admit that I am impressed.'

It was quite ingenious. That was for certain.

The maintenance guy was shuffling his fete like a child in need of a restroom. 'Can I go now?' he asked. 'Only there's a problem with the plumbing on the fifth floor. A tank is overflowing and the longer I leave it, the more likely it is the overflow will back up and then we have a flood.'

Lena dismissed him without looking up. 'Of course, Bernhard, please go. Thank you for helping.'

Opening the bag for me to see inside, Lena pulled out a lady's sapphire ring. 'I think she hit more than just the ambassador's room tonight.' Reaching back inside, she then pulled out a diamond necklace and my eyes nearly popped out of my head.

'That's mine!' I screeched. But before I could say anything else, a jolt of adrenalin hit my bloodstream and I panicked. 'We have to get back to my suite!' I was already running to the door.

I flew out of the door and started running along the corridor. I needed to find the nearest elevator, but I didn't know where that was.

Barbie caught up to me easily. 'What is it, Patty?'

I shot her a worried look. 'That was in my bedroom when I got changed to attend the banquet.' When she didn't get my point straight away, I yelled, 'We left Molly in there!'

Molly

I 'd brought my teenage housemaid with me because there was a slim, yet very real, danger that the Godmother might target her to get at me. In the opinion of the police, anyone connected to me could be a target. I doubted anyone would bother with my maid, but I wasn't taking any chances.

Now I worried I'd left her to fight off a thief who might also be a killer. I worried for my dogs too. Anna was stupidly brave; willing to take on anyone and stand her ground. What would she make of an intruder? Would she think Molly to be threatened? She'd met Martha earlier when she was pretending to be Andrea, so perhaps Anna would choose to be friendly. I could believe that, but not if Molly woke up and attempted to stop the thief.

Terrified for what I might find, I ran along the hallway to my suite's door. Passing mirrors, exquisite oil paintings, and large exotic potted plants, and surrounded by an entourage, I arrived at my door, out of breath and clutching the entry key card in my hand.

I didn't even get inside before I saw the spots of blood on the carpet outside.

My head swam as I opened the door and it was only Jermaine's steadying hand that kept me on my feet. Wayne pushed by me and ran to my bedroom.

Spots of blood ran in a trail from my bedroom door to the exit. There wasn't much of it, but there was quite enough to freak me out. That neither dog had barked or run out to find me could only mean one thing and I couldn't even articulate it in my head.

With my head resting against Jermaine's chest, a yell of shock from Molly brought my head up and spun me around. An explosion of expletives, mostly from Molly, but plenty from Wayne too, came with an accompanying sound of someone hitting someone else.

Barbie's eyes flared as she sprinted after Lena, Rosie, and the other security guards. Jermaine and I went too but I was not prepared for the sight I found.

Molly was standing on the bed wearing just her bra and knickers, she had her fists up ready to fight but there was no threat to her: Wayne was on the carpet cupping his testicles. 'She punched me in the nuts,' he hissed through tightly clenched teeth.

'Yeah? Try to grab me again mister and see what you get next time!' Molly shouted at him. 'No means no!'

'I was checking your pulse,' he gasped and rolled to one side, curling into a foetal position and whimpering.

There was more blood on the carpet by my dressing table, but still no sign of the dogs.

'What happened here, Molly?' I begged, still fearful, but now also quite confused.

Molly looked up, and as if for the first time, realised there were several men looking at her. She made eye contact with me and looked ashamedly down at the bed. 'Sorry, Mrs Fisher. I woke up feeling groggy and still in that ballgown you bought me.' We could see it discarded next to the bed. 'I didn't realise I was in your bed, so I stripped off and went back to sleep. Then creepy creeper guy tried to grab me, and I hit him, and then you all ran in.'

'I was checking your pulse,' Wayne insisted weakly from the carpet.

Moving to the dressing table, I checked my jewellery box and found it empty. Martha had been in here and she robbed me without Molly even waking up. 'Where are the dogs, Molly?' I asked. I got a blank look in response, but when I called, 'Anna?' A yip came from the corner of the room.

The blood on my carpet had to be from her. Not her blood, I don't mean that, but she had a habit for attacking ankles and she could be vicious if she wanted to.

Barbie was nearest to the yipping sound which came from my bathroom. I hadn't thought to check there because the door was open, but Barbie went in and came out again a second later with the laundry hamper in her hands. Inside were two angry dachshund faces and there were traces of deep red around Anna's jowls.

Barbie placed the laundry basket on its side no the bed so the girls could walk out. I checked them both over. 'Goodness, girls, have you had an adventure?' I asked them, getting kisses in return when I put my face close enough.

Molly spotted the blood on the carpet. 'Have I missed something?' she asked.

Regroup

I knew I shouldn't be drinking another gin, but my fluctuating heart rate demanded it. Spread around the couches and chairs in my suite's wide living space, the team were taking a moment to regroup.

Anna and Georgie were asleep on my lap, neither dog caring to dwell on the recent past. Wayne was upright again though he still looked tender, and most of us were drinking gin. From the security team, Lena led the charge on the alcohol front, but even though she was theoretically off duty and could excuse herself having quit less than an hour ago, Rosie soon followed suit and the guys' resistance crumbled the moment she did.

Molly asked for one and got a stern look from Jermaine, swiftly followed by a black coffee which she meekly took.

Only Barbie abstained, nervous energy making her bounce on the spot. 'What do we know so far, Patty?' she asked. 'Come on, that itchy brain of yours must have got this almost worked out by now.'

I wished it had.

'We've found our thief,' said Rosie. 'That's a good start.'

'Only for you,' I pointed out. 'I need to find the killer and though they may be one and the same, we haven't actually found the thief, all we've done is identify who it is.' That might be viewed as a pedantic point by some, but I felt it was important enough to clarify. That the jewels were still in the building and hadn't been collected yet told me Martha was still here too. That made her braver than I expected, or perhaps more arrogant. She came close to getting caught earlier and yet she came back to steal from me. Maybe she figured the security team would piece enough parts together to question why she'd been in the ambassador's suite and that would be the end of her winning streak. She must have stolen millions in jewels and other items already, why not grab a few more if you think this is your last chance?

'Who is on the list, madam?' asked Jermaine.

It was a good question because it prompted me to lay out my thoughts. 'We know Martha was in his room and that she robbed him. The ambassador's aide/lover is missing so I think we can assume he is also dead. When we catch up to Martha, we can find out more about what she saw and what she did, but I cannot rule out political motivation. I don't think Martha is the killer; she screamed when she saw the body.'

'You think the Itarnians might be behind it?' asked Barbie. 'That General Armand looked capable.'

She wasn't wrong. General Armand has the most to gain some might say, but his behaviour when he came into the ambassador's suite confused me. If he organised the murder and was there to reveal the ambassador's death, why did he let Jermaine's nakedness put him off?' I blew out a tired sigh. 'It could be one of the Zangrabarians too. According to the foreign minister, the entire peace treaty is a house of cards. It could come tumbling down at any point because at a cellular level the two nations do not trust each other. They have agreed to split a piece of land that tens of thousands from each side have died fighting over. Any one of the Royal Guard or the Itarnian forces here tonight could bear a grudge and feel a need to settle it violently. All it will take is one fight and we already have a dead ambassador and a missing Itarnian soldier.'

Lena grimaced. 'I sure hope he doesn't turn up dead.'

Around the room, all the radios squawked at once. 'This is Hingis,' their boss growled. 'I want everyone in the control room now.'

None of them hesitated, but I noticed Rosie chose to empty her glass of gin before she put it down. Lena stayed where she was. 'Stay in contact,' she shouted as her team ran for the door.

'What do we do?' asked Barbie.

Looking her dead in the face, I said, 'We spy.'

She bit her lip, looking nervous. 'Who are we going to spy on, Patty?'

Sucking in a breath to settle my nerves, I gave her my answer, 'Everyone.'

For me, the approach to this mystery was getting simpler. There was a huge pool of potential suspects with a few likely ones right at the top. The security team were looking for Martha and the Itarnians were looking for their missing man. Sooner or later, I felt certain one or both would be successful and there wasn't much point in throwing our efforts into finding them first. No one was looking for the missing ambassador's aide, which gave me a task we could pursue, but I couldn't help but question what the Maharaja and his top soldier, General Farhoud, were up to, and what were the Itarnians saying when no one was there to hear them. Because I knew almost nothing and had almost no clues to follow, I was going to watch them all.

Putting Lena on the spot, I wanted to know, 'Can you pose as yourself and join the Itarnians looking for their missing soldier?'

She looked surprised at the request. 'Um, sure, yes. You want me to just see what they are doing and report back?'

'We need someone on the inside,' I nodded. They won't talk freely with you there, but they also won't know you quit earlier and you are still in uniform so unless you run into Hingis or someone loyal to him, you can at least know what they are up to.'

'I'll do my best.' She went to a mirror to check her appearance, tightened her ponytail, and brushed some lint from her jacket.

Facing David, Wayne, and my friends, I told them, 'I'm going to take the Maharaja. He'll be expecting an update from me, I'm sure, so I'll give him that and try to get a feel for what is going on in his camp.'

'Surely you don't suspect him, Patty?' Barbie said, her face a frown. 'He's the one who gave you the house. He's the one who invited you here.'

I tilted my head as a sort of half shrug. 'He's also the third richest man on the planet for a reason. Would he agree to share all that potential mineral wealth? The planet's geography and boundaries have been shaped by the greed of man for as long as he could pick up a weapon and use it to get that which he coveted. His arrival at the ambassador's room was conveniently timed too.'

'That could be just coincidence, Patty,' Barbie argued.

I didn't disagree. 'It could be. Or, if one chooses to be paranoid, one could suggest that he singled me out and got me here tonight so he could put me in the suite opposite the man he intended to have murdered. Instantly involved, he then asks me to head up the investigation knowing full well that I wouldn't say no. He gets to claim to the world he has done everything he can to ensure peace, provides a patsy somehow, blames the Itarnians for restarting the war, and invades them to claim the land almost unopposed because the Itarnian forces have pulled back to their border.'

'This is way too complicated for me,' said Molly, looking up from her phone for the first time since we'd sat down.

Barbie's hands were held to her face in horror. 'But he's such a sweet young man.'

'He's also a teenager with an army at his disposal. Look, I'm not saying that is what is happening here. It's just one possible scenario.' I prayed to God I was completely wrong because if the Maharaja was behind it, the logical way to ensure he doesn't get caught would be to kill me if I even get a sniff of the truth.

Jermaine finished wiping down the counter where he made drinks and tidied away the empty glasses. 'If you are to speak with the Maharaja and Miss Glauser is to spy on the Itarnians, what should the rest of us do?'

Something had occurred to me while I was thinking about the lack of clues, and someone needed to check it out.

'I'm going where you go, Mrs Fisher,' insisted Wayne. 'That is the only reason I am here. My job is to protect you from any threat the Godmother might make.' Actually, I was more inclined to believe the task appointed by Scotland Yard was to watch me and see if he could pick up a trail back to the Godmother next time she tried to kill me, but I didn't say that.

Jermaine huffed but didn't say anything. Protecting me was his job and always had been, but he and I discussed that this situation might occur when Wayne first appeared. He wasn't happy about it, but he would allow it to happen.

To Barbie and Jermaine, I said, 'Can you check on something?'

Spying

We departed in different directions, Barbie and Jermaine following Lena's instructions on where to go, Lena taking the stairs, and myself with Wayne getting into the elevator yet again. We left Molly to look after the dogs and made sure she locked the door from the inside just in case. David planned to return to the party. Actually, he wanted to stick by my side and help me, but I insisted that for now, I would be able to move faster and think more clearly, if left by myself.

In the quiet of the steel box, Wayne said, 'You trust Jermaine implicitly.' It was a statement not a question.

I nodded without turning around to look at him. 'He and I have been through quite a bit together. He has saved my life several times.'

'Good.' I thought that might be all he had to say on the subject but as we neared the banquet floor and the car slowed, he said,

'I'm better.' I shot him a look over my shoulder. 'I'm certain he is very well trained. One need only look at the way he holds himself and moves to know he is capable. I am glad you have had such good protection thus far and I understand if you might now feel exposed without him nearby. Which is why I want to assure you that I am better.'

Accepting what he claimed and hoping that it wasn't just a boastful display of ego, I stepped through the elevator doors as they opened. The sound of music drifted out from the banquet hall as it had before, drawing me in and giving me a false sense that all was fine when I knew it was not. Expecting to see empty seats where guests might have nervously abandoned the banquet to go to their rooms or attempt to leave, I was surprised to find very few without an occupant. With Wayne as my shadow, looking confident and dangerous in his black dinner jacket, I worked my way around the outside of the room and up to the top table.

Sitting on a slightly raised dais, one would have to clamber onto it from any approach vector but the rear where there were members of the Maharaja's Royal Guard to control access.

I was recognised fortunately and welcomed forward quickly by the Maharaja when his guards alerted him that I was drawing near. Showing how much he respected me, the Maharaja jumped to his feet to greet me rather than wait for me to get to him.

'Mrs Fisher, have you any news? Things have not gone well here tonight as you might be able to tell by the absence of the Itarnian party. I have left General Armand to cool off but must attempt to reconcile again shortly.' He looked genuinely nervous for how things might turn out. 'One of his men has gone missing,' he told me soto voce.

'Yes, Your Highness, I am aware.'

He looked surprised for a second before laughing. 'Of course, Mrs Fisher. How could you not already know? It may never cease to amaze me how you know more about what is going on than any one I have ever met.'

He guided me to a table where he held a chair for me to sit. Wayne crossed his hands behind his back and watched the room from behind me. 'I have my own team involved in the search, Your Highness, but I do have some news.' This was the part where I lied through my teeth. I needed to see how he might react. 'I have uncovered a plot to kill the ambassador, but you will not like what I have to say.'

He frowned in confusion. 'The Itarnians came here with a deliberate plan to kill their own ambassador? You can prove that?'

Keeping my eyes locked on his, I said, 'No, Your Highness, I believe the assassination,' I used the controversial word deliberately, 'was planned and executed by Zangrabar.' My tactic was intended to shortcut the discovery process so I could find out if he knew anything about such a plot quickly. I believed he would reveal the truth with his eyes, which he did: he had no idea.

His eyes widened in shock at my revelation and his mouth opened though he caught it before his jaw fell and snapped it closed. I could see his mind working: he believed my claim, and he believed he might know who among his people here might be guilty.

I felt enormous relief that he wasn't complicit though I now worried that my ruse might prove to be a false tip that would send him to accuse someone who was equally innocent. 'Your Highness, I must confess that I know of no such plot. I made that up to see how you might react. There are now three people missing in this hotel, two of whom are directly associated with the ambassador. I apologise for my subterfuge, yet I felt it was necessary to achieve the result you desire in such a short space of time.'

He looked angry at my lies, but as quickly as the emotion arose, he pushed it away. He was a king indeed: always in control. Begging a moment's grace, he leaned to his side and motioned for an aide. Aladdin stepped forward, bending from the waist to place his ear close to the Maharaja's mouth where the instruction given, whatever it was, could not be heard.

Aladdin departed on his master's command and the king brought his attention back to me. 'I fear, Mrs Fisher, that your lie may have some truth to it. I can say no more at this time, yet I urge you to explore the concept that one of my own guard may be responsible. They are all hand-picked, however it is not a perfect process.'

'I understand, Your Highness. Can you tell me anything more?'

His answer was interrupted by the arrival of a contingent of his Royal Guard. They looked to be on high alert, and I had to wonder what news they carried. The captain stopped the guard just short of the dais to come forward alone. 'Your

Majesty.' He bowed his head. 'I must remove you from the room for your own safety. Please come with me, sire.'

It was not a request, even though it sounded like one, and it reminded me of movies where someone takes a shot at the American President and the Secret Service run him from the room with a wall of bodies to protect him.

'Please excuse me, Mrs Fisher,' he said as he got up.

There was no time for anything else, the Maharaja was already being led away, but as they left the table, I heard the captain say, 'The missing Itarnian solider has been found, sire. He's been strangled.'

The news ought not to have shocked me, but it did. Of the three misplaced persons, I expected the soldier to be the one who turned up having simply taken a wrong turn coming out of the gents or something. Not only was he dead, but he'd been murdered since it is physically impossible to strangle oneself. General Armand would know about it any second, if he didn't already, and that might mean finding the Ambassador's killer was a moot point.

Moments after the Maharaja departed, surrounded by his Royal Guard, the Itarnian General swept back into the room leading his entourage of angry looking soldiers.

'We should move, Mrs Fisher,' said Wayne, leaning down to speak quietly. I was sitting in the missing ambassador's seat but chose to remain where I was. I doubted I could make things worse, but maybe I could make them better with a little truth. He would find out about the ambassador sooner or later, and perhaps I could manage his reaction to that news by delivering it willingly.

Standing to greet the Itarnian general, my desire to prevent war was scuppered by the appearance of Mr Hingis, the hotel manager. He positioned himself directly in front of the general's path and before I, or anyone else, could stop him, he had his ear.

'General Armand, my name is Franco Hingis. I am the Exclusive's manager. I feel duty bound to inform you of a development I believe has been hidden from you.' The general stopped advancing, suddenly keen to hear what Hingis had to say.

The Itarnian troops formed a mass behind their general and from behind them came Lena's voice. 'No, Hingis! Are you mad?'

I was hurrying now, running to get to them and could see the thunder forming on Hingis's brow. 'What are you still doing here, Glauser? I fired you an hour ago.'

She ignored his question, rushing around the soldiers to get to her former boss. 'You are about to create an incident, Hingis. Think it through, man,' she begged.

'What is going on?' General Armand demanded to know. 'This woman claimed you had assigned her to be our liaison as we searched for our missing man. Are you telling me she was spying instead? And what is this development that's been hidden from me?'

Before anyone could stop him, not that it was possible to stop the news now without shooting Hingis, he gave General Armand the piece of information we all desperately wanted to keep secret until we knew more. 'Ambassador Hosseini is dead. He was murdered earlier this evening.'

If a cartoonist attempted to capture the moment the news reached General Armand, he would need to draw a mushroom cloud above his head. He grabbed Hingis by the throat, startling the hotel manager, who for some reason, wasn't expecting the news to be taken badly.

'What do you mean the ambassador is dead?' snarled General Armand, his face an inch from Hingis's. 'How long ago did this happen?'

Around the pair, the Exclusive's security team all put a hand on their sidearms as the Itarnian contingent of soldiers moved in to back their general. All the weapons remained in their holsters and no one attempted to get Hingis free. 'We don't know,' squeaked Hingis, his larynx being squeezed to make speaking difficult. 'His body was found in his suite earlier this evening.'

'What!' General Armand looked like he might explode in anger, his rage level was so high. 'I am just hearing about this now!'

'I ordered Glauser to inform you,' Hingis squeaked, pawing at the general's hand on his throat. 'I fired her because she failed to do so.'

'You didn't fire me,' Lena argued. 'I quit because you are a coward and an idiot.'

General Armand nodded. 'She's right. You are a coward. If you are her boss, then it was your task to inform me, not hers.' He thrust Hingis away, throwing him backwards so he sprawled on the floor. Then the general swept his eyes to look at the dais, which was now all but devoid of guests and raised his voice to shout, 'Where is he?' he demanded. Around the banquet hall, guests showed their good sense and began to escape. 'Where is the boy who thinks himself a king?'

I was glad the Maharaja wasn't here to hear the general's insults as they were cause for war in themselves.

The general raised his hand toward Lena, about to attack her for her part in the deception, but I was able to get in first. 'Since your ambassador's body was discovered, the Maharaja has been doing all he can to discover the killer's identity. He is not to blame, but I wonder, General, if you are?'

It was an open insult, delivered knowingly because it made everyone present draw a shocked breath. He spun around to face his accuser and found me standing my ground. My knees were shaking but I looked him in the eye, nevertheless.

'You dare to accuse me?' he growled. His aide-de-camp wanted to get around him to physically attack me even though Agent Garrett stood by my shoulder ready to repel anyone who might try.

I took a slow breath through my nose and held his gaze. When I was ready to speak, I said, 'Good evening, General Armand. My name is Patricia Fisher.' He gawped at me incredulously for a moment, glanced at his aide-de-camp and then back at me. 'Who stands to gain, General? I am certain you must recognise my name so I shall skip the formalities and tell you what has been happening.'

Hingis scrambled back a few feet to find two of the Exclusive's guards who helped him regain his feet. He looked like he wanted to stop me from talking but he had enough sense to keep quiet.

'The ambassador was found dead in his suite earlier this evening as the hotel manager has revealed. An investigation is already underway to determine the killer's identity, but the question I always start with is: Who stands to gain? In this case, you do, General. With the war ended, you are essentially out of a job, are you not? You have no love for your neighbour, that is perfectly clear, and find the ambassador's sexual preferences wholly distasteful. That you could be responsible for his death is entirely plausible. Equally, it could be many others, but the hotel has been sealed until special investigators from the Swiss embassy can get here. Isn't that right, Mr Hingis?'

Hingis nodded his head nervously.

'The Exclusive is sealed?' raged the general, each new revelation making him yet angrier than the one before. 'You think you can keep me captive here? My men will smash their way out if that is what is necessary to ensure my safety.'

Praying I could instigate calm, I said, 'General Armand, the killer could be among your troops. I beg that you allow the investigation to proceed and assist us by having your delegation answer some questions. Someone in this hotel killed your ambassador. His aide, Behrouz Parastui, is missing. The woman who found the ambassador's body is missing, and one of your own men went missing and has been found dead. All this has occurred in the last few hours. There is a killer at large and he cannot be allowed to escape.'

His eyes, which ought to not have been able to flare any wider, suddenly did exactly that. He wasn't of a mind to listen to a woman. 'This is the lowest insult yet. The Maharaja's men kill one of my soldiers and he leaves a woman to address me as if she is my equal. If we were in my country, I would have you flogged.'

'How wonderfully forward thinking Itarnia must be,' said Wayne, diverting the general's attention away from me for a second.

I added, 'We are not in your country, General. Theoretically, we are in Switzerland. So that being the case, we are equals, and I need your help to find the killer. Will you let me see your soldier's body, please?'

He shook his head. 'The Maharaja is to blame for the ambassador's death, no one else. I do not need to conduct an investigation to discover what I already know to be true. No doubt he arranged for Behrouz Parastui to be killed also and then killed the woman because she saw something she should not have. I am his ultimate target. He lured me here so he could remove me from the chessboard. I will contact my embassy and they will storm this hotel if you do not open the doors. The bloodshed will be on the Maharaja's hands.' I believed he meant it, and he dismissed me with his back as he turned around to leave the room. His troops went with him, but his aide-de-camp hung on for just a brief moment, eyeing me curiously before he too swept from the banquet room.

'That could have gone better,' I mumbled to myself and scratched my head.

Wayne moved around to stand in front of me. 'We have to consider that there simply isn't time to solve this case, Mrs Fisher. The special investigators will arrive soon, I am sure, and it is their job, not yours. You have no authority to question the Itarnians, or anyone else for that matter. We can keep going, I know you made a promise to the Maharaja to do what you could, but there is a limit to what can be achieved in such a short space of time.' He was trying to make me feel better about how much of a mess we were making, but his words were overheard by someone else, who chose to comment.

'Young man, you clearly don't know Patricia Fisher like I do.'

I almost screamed with shock at the sound of the familiar voice, spinning around in a flash so my eyes could confirm what my ears were telling me.

Surprise Guests

S huffling up behind me were two retired Hawaiian cops who I'd last seen in Zangrabar and behind them were the two women I'd left them with.

'Rick! Akamu! What are you doing here?' I squealed and wrapped them both into a hug. With an arm around their necks, they both hugged me back. Rick was Caucasian and Akamu Polynesian, but both about the same age and the same shape, which is to say a little rotund. They were short too at around five feet seven or eight, but they were in their seventies so had most likely been taller as younger men.

'We hitched a lift with the Maharaja,' said Rick, a beaming smile on his face. 'He had a bunch of private jets coming this way.'

'Yeah,' said Akamu. 'We just asked one of the royal guard to pass a message when we heard he had this big trip to London planned. He was going to be here for a few days, and we figured we could meet up with you.'

Rick chuckled as he took over telling the story. 'So then this courier turns up at our place asking that we attend the banquet tonight. The Maharaja has a touch for the dramatics it seems because he asked us to keep it a secret so he could surprise you.'

Akamu's face took on a serious expression. 'It looks to me like something went wrong though. Did I hear that the ambassador was murdered?'

'Yeah, we've been watching you run back and forth all night,' added Rick. 'I thought we were never going to catch your eye.'

I nodded ruefully. 'The ambassador was killed some time this afternoon, or possibly in the very early evening. The whole thing is a terrible mess. I have to find out who did it and pray it wasn't one of the Zangrabarians because ...'

'They'll be straight back to killing each other,' Rick concluded sadly.

They hadn't been able to get a word in until now, but Agnes and Mavis waved a hello as the conversation reached a lull. They looked good with tans and both had gained a couple of pounds as they relaxed into a more homebound lifestyle. They were in their sixties and both attractive women.

I shook my head at the surprise of seeing them, then remembered the policeman standing two feet away. 'Everyone, this is Agent Garrett of Scotland Yard.' I saw the girls' eyes widen. 'Wayne, sweetie, could you be a dear and get me some water?'

His expression registered surprise for a moment, but he said, 'Sure, okay. You want sparkling or still?'

'Sparkling would be lovely, thank you so much.' As soon as he moved out of earshot, I hissed, 'Aren't you two still wanted by half the law enforcement agencies on the planet? How did you get into England without being arrested?'

Agnes smirked. 'Fake passports, sweetie. We've been in Zangrabar for months, Patricia. It didn't take us long to find the required underworld contacts.'

Both the men shared a look. They'd met the girls on board the Aurelia when they were robbing people and we caught them. The guys were retired Hawaiian cops and their girlfriends were career criminals who had operated various scams and schemes all over the world to support a luxurious lifestyle few, other than the superrich, ever glimpse. Then they'd put their lives on the line to help us defeat terrorists with a biological weapon, surrendered to the authorities, escaped, and then returned to rescue the guys when they were wrongfully arrested as part of a conspiracy in Zangrabar.

Rick and Akamu, both widowers for many years, developed a soft spot for the thieves and were doing their best to turn a blind eye to their nefarious past provided they behaved themselves now. The pair of couples chose to stay in Zangrabar due to its lack of extradition treaty should the girls ever be discovered. Plus, because all four played a part in rescuing the Maharaja, they were accorded hero status, free accommodation, and a host of other benefits.

Seeing friends I'd said goodbye to and imagined I might never see again filled my heart, but it also gave me some ideas.

'Guys I have to work out who killed the ambassador before the situation here reaches critical mass. The Itarnians are going to try to leave and will be stopped by the Exclusive's security team but that won't calm things down. If anything, it will make General Armand even more desperate to take action. He might look to take on the Zangrabarian royal guard hand to hand, just to see that hostilities get restarted. He might even try to take the Maharaja hostage and he threatened to bring forces here from his own embassy where they will undoubtedly have weapons. The only way to defuse this now is to present the killer and pray that's enough.'

Rick asked. 'What do you need us to do?'

I looked around for a chair and took the weight off my legs as I thought about what my next step should be. 'I don't have much to go on, guys. There are no clues to follow but there is a body I want to get a look at.'

'A body?' repeated Akamu, questioningly.

'Yes,' I nodded grimly. Then with a wry smile, I said, 'I'm going to need a distraction.'

Rich and Akamu grinned at each other. 'Those are our speciality,' chuckled Rick.

Behind them, Mavis and Agnes rolled their eyes, but I needed their help too. I explained my thoughts and asked their opinion. I knew they would help me no matter how daft my ideas were, but the girls had an even better idea than the one I came up with, they just needed to find the kitchen and a few minutes to get ready.

When they departed, I called Barbie.

'Hey, Patty. You were right, but it took us three attempts to find the right one and she was long gone by the time we got there.' With some advice on locations from Lena, I'd sent Barbie and Jermaine to look for places where the Exclusive had medical supplies or first aid kits stashed. If Anna had cut Martha's ankle badly enough that she was leaving a blood trail, then she would need to dress the wound. However, with people looking for her, Martha would seek the most obscure place to go which was why it took Jermaine and Barbie three attempts to find it.

Martha was still in the hotel somewhere, that much I was certain of, and I was unable to work out what her escape plan might be. Now that her crimes were discovered, the only sensible course was for her to exit with her stolen goods – she didn't know we'd stolen them back yet – and then never return. But the ambassador's murder meant the Exclusive's exits were sealed. I didn't think she had a secret exit no one else knew about. The fake electrical panel was one thing; it was a tiny aperture to pass a small bag through. People would notice an entire door.

'I'm in the banquet room, Barbie. You and Jermaine might as well come back to me here. I have a surprise waiting for you,' I said teasingly rather than tell her about the old friends who'd just surprised me.

When I placed my phone back into my handbag, Wayne asked, 'What are you planning to do, Mrs Fisher?' He'd found me a bottle of sparkling water and then found a glass and ice; he was such a nice man. The banquet room was now almost devoid of guests; once the first few departed, the others followed, but a few remained still. Perhaps they had nowhere to go.

I couldn't get on with anything else, so I took a moment to articulate my thoughts to the policeman. 'There are, or rather were, three missing people. One of them has shown up dead and that's the second body today already. The important question I want an answer to is whether they were killed by the same person. I think the ambassador's aide Behrouz Parastui is also dead, but the killers either took his body with them or knocked him out and took him elsewhere to make the kill.'

Wayne interrupted, 'Wait. You said killers. You think there is more than one person?'

'I'm leaning that way. If Behrouz's body, dead or alive, was taken away, which I assume it was because he's not there and we cannot find him, then that is not a task for one person.'

Wayne argued, 'What about a cleaning trolley? He could have been stuffed into one of those by the killer and wheeled away.'

I had to concede the point. 'Yes. It would also mean they could be seen by other people without risk that the body might be spotted. Good thinking.' Why hadn't I thought of that? 'Anyway, until we can find the missing thief or the missing ambassador's assistant, I don't have much to go on so I want to see the dead Itarnian soldier. General Armand is disinclined to let me, so I must resort to more ... extreme means.'

'Do you know where the Itarnians are?' Wayne asked.

'Not yet.' To find out, I called Lena.

'Mrs Fisher is that you?' her voice came down the line sounding out of breath. 'Would you believe that idiot Hingis begged me to take my job back and put me in charge of dealing with the Itarnians? I thought they were genuinely going to start a riot and break out of the building.'

'Where are they now?'

She took a deep breath to recover. 'I thought they were going to rush us. If they had, they most likely would have overpowered us, but their general ordered them to stand down. For a moment I thought it was over, but General Armand then announced that he has armed soldiers coming to us from his embassy. I think they mean to storm the hotel like it's some kind of hostage rescue. The special investigators are on route from Switzerland by private jet, but they won't be here for another two hours. This will all be long over by then. We have no protocol for this kind of scenario. If we get shot at, I'm not sure what I am supposed to do.'

'I might be able to help with that, Lena. You need to tell me where they are though,' I reminded her since she didn't answer the question the first time.

'Oh, yes, sorry. They are all in a conference room on the first floor where they can see the front approach to the hotel. I think they plan to wait there until they see their soldiers and then attack the lobby guards from two sides.'

'Where are you, Lena? I might need some help.'

'In the lobby. I just got back here.'

'Okay. If I can help, I will. Good luck.'

I moved my thumb to end the call, but she yelled for me to wait, 'Mrs Fisher you said you might be able to help. What are you going to do?'

Rick and Akamu shuffled back into the banquet hall with the girls in tow. Agnes had a bucket in her right hand. I sucked a breath between my teeth. 'Something stupid, Lena. Something stupid. Just tell your guards to ignore any alarms and anything they see happening near that first-floor conference room.' I cut her off quickly before she could ask me more questions. Then I looked at the bucket. 'What's that?' I asked, wondering if I really wanted to know the answer.

Agnes had a wicked smile. 'It's a chemical concoction that will make a whole load of white mist. It's a bit like dry ice and totally harmless but it will scare anyone who sees it.'

Wayne raised an eyebrow.

As she came nearer, I peered into the bucket where a pool of liquid swirled. It didn't look like much. 'Is that ice?' I enquired, seeing squarish chunks floating about.

Agnes looked down at her bucket. 'Yup. It's a mix of household chemicals. When the ice melts, which it is starting to, the water reacts with the mix to create a gas. Now we just need to get it into the ventilation duct that leads to the people you want to scare.'

'We just need a distraction to draw everyone away from the area where they have the guard. This should work perfectly,' I added, biting my lip in thought as I silently questioned whether this really would work or was just plain nuts.

'Guys!' Barbie had arrived. Rick, Akamu and the girls turned to see her running across the banquet room. Her dress barely contained her large, bulbous breasts, which now jiggled up and down as she pranced toward us.

'Goodness,' murmured Rick, 'I'd forgotten about those.'

'Yeah, they really do have a life of their own, don't they?' agreed Akamu.

Snippily Mavis asked, 'Spotted something you like, boys?'

Both men took to looking at the floor or the ceiling or anywhere but Barbie's bouncing boobs.

'Oh, wow, guys!' Barbie wrapped both men into a hug, squashing their faces against her chest since she was six inches taller than them in her high heels. Neither man fought her off. Then she released them to greet Agnes and Mavis as well. 'Wow,' she repeated. 'What are you all doing here? Why didn't you say you were coming?'

Jermaine arrived too, his pace more sedate and his greeting equally so as he shook hands with our friends.

'They wanted to surprise us,' I told her. 'Now they are going to help us. Oh, wait, you don't know about the Itarnian guard, do you?' I spent the next two minutes telling Barbie and Jermaine about what they missed and my plan to get a look at the body.

'What do you hope to learn, Mrs Fisher?' asked Wayne. He wasn't trying to stop us, but he didn't look happy about the plan either and the bucket of ice was beginning to seep mist onto the floor.

I started walking; time was not our friend. 'I hope to find a clue to why the soldier is dead. It might be a long shot, but I know one thing for certain, Agent Garrett.'

Yielding to my hook, he asked, 'What's that?'

'A person misses every shot they don't take.'

Taking a Shot

The elevator pinged and the doors swished open. With a hand on the edge of the car to stop the door from closing, I leaned out to take a look. The Itarnians had two soldiers posted outside the conference room. I had to assume General Armand, his aide-de-camp, and the rest of the soldiers were all inside, but the two men eyed me suspiciously when I poked my head around the corner to look their way. I was checking their position, or rather, the position of the conference room so I could get it right and not gas an empty room by mistake. Wayne was with me, insisting he stay close to me but also giving a second opinion on the whereabouts of the room.

The doors to the conference room were solid wood so I wouldn't be able to see inside even if I went along the corridor to them, but I was content enough to let the plan start. With a single step taking me back inside the elevator, I travelled back up one floor to where the team now waited for my return.

As we re-joined them, Wayne said, 'I just want to say, for the record, that I think this is the wrong thing to do. We should wait for the Swiss special investigators to get here and let them handle it. This is not our problem.' Everyone in the group turned to look at Wayne with frowns on their faces. 'I cannot be a part of this,' he added defensively.

Rick, Akamu, and possibly Barbie were about to tear a strip off him, but I tried to understand his position. 'That's okay, Wayne. You're right. As a law enforcement officer, you shouldn't get involved. Maybe you want to wait outside?'

He didn't move. 'I need to keep you in sight, Mrs Fisher. In sight at all times were my orders.'

'Very well.' I switched my attention back to what Agnes and Mavis were doing. They had a portion of the floor up already. Like a lot of modern buildings, the floor in the functional areas was carpet tile over a dummy floor that allowed cable and ducting to pass underneath. Getting access to it took seconds.

Mavis manoeuvred the bucket. 'The gas is heavier than air. All I need to do now is find an air duct into the room below, add some water, and stand back.'

'What do we do about the two guards outside the room?' asked Barbie.

'We shouldn't have to do anything,' I explained. 'When the gas starts hitting the room,' I nodded to Agnes who added the water. Clouds of thick white mist started broiling up and over the sides of the bucket as the home-made gas billowed out and down into the floor, 'the Itarnians will run, but in the confusion, we will be able to get in and grab the body. We should at least have enough time to examine it quickly.'

'This really is a long shot, madam,' Jermaine said with a frown. 'What if they don't run away? Or what if they take the body with them?'

'Then we try something different. All I know is, we are stuck here, and I feel I must try to solve this. I promised the Maharaja I would.'

Agnes checked her watch. 'This stuff will only take a few seconds to fill the room downstairs. We'd better get going if you want to time your entry with their exit.'

Thinking the elevator might take too long, those of us not in our sixties and seventies, ran down the stairs, but cautiously opening the door to the first floor, I spied the same two Itarnian soldiers still outside the conference room doors and looking just as bored as they had before.

'Did it not work?' whispered Barbie, leaning over the top of me to peer through the gap as well.

'Maybe. I don't know. They didn't go running for cover like we expected. Maybe it didn't go through the air vent. Maybe it went somewhere else.'

'Could you have got the position of the room wrong, madam?' asked Jermaine.

It was a fair question since nothing appeared to have happened. All I could do was shrug, but a bong from the direction of the elevators drew the guards' attention just before Rick, Akamu, Agnes, and Mavis shuffled into sight.

'What are they doing?' I asked. I didn't expect an answer, of course. I was merely voicing my confusion.

Mavis walked right up to the nearest guard. 'Young fellow, I think you should check on your friends inside the room.'

The guard scowled down at her. He was in his late twenties and had the look and shape of a professional soldier. 'They are fine. Go away.'

He spoke good English, even though it came out with an accent, but Mavis persisted. 'I doubt they are. I just dropped a whole load of knock-out gas on them. Perhaps you should just check.'

He narrowed his eyes at her. It was a good line, saying she'd used knock out gas, but I couldn't see what she hoped to achieve: the gas hadn't made them run away as we hoped they might.

Overcome by curiosity, the soldier Mavis hadn't spoken to, cracked the door just a little to glance inside. We could only see the back of his head from our position, but we all saw his body spasm when he looked inside. He shouted something in his mother language and shoved his way through the door. A small cloud of gas escaped the gap in the door which made Agnes put her arms out to either side as she stepped away from it, pushing her friends back in the process.

I skewed my lips to one side in wonder. What had she done?

The first soldier's shouts drew his colleague inside as well, both men vanishing through the door as yet more white gas floated out. It wasn't at floor height as Agnes previously described and as we watched, the two girls grabbed the doors and yanked them shut again, trapping the men inside along with all the gas as they both visibly held their breath and waved their arms to drive the gas away.

Intrigue forcing my feet to move, I pulled the stair door fully open and came into the corridor. Rick saw me and waved with one hand as he fanned the air with the other. 'What's going on?' I asked.

'Got to give the gas a little time to work on the two guards,' he told me. 'Think that will do it?' He asked Agnes.

She nodded, checked around to make sure the escaped gas had dissipated, then let go of the breath she'd been holding. After gasping a fresh lungful of oxygen, she said, 'I think that since neither guard tried to get out, we can be safely assured they are all dead.'

My jaw dropped.

'Only kidding,' she laughed. 'It's just knock-out gas. They'll all be sleeping like babies. I couldn't use the kind of gas that kills people. Rick would never allow it.' Honestly, I think her boyfriend's disapproval might be the only reason she didn't use killer gas.

Nevertheless, I had to shake my head in wonder. 'You said it would scare them and make them run away.'

Agnes squinted at me. 'If I told you I was making gas that induces unconsciousness, would you have let me do it?'

She had a point. 'No, probably not.' Then she grabbed the doors. 'Now, everyone hold your breath.' She and Agnes threw the doors inwards, creating a swirling vortex of cloud-like mist inside the room.

The entire Itarnian party were out cold. Every last one of them was unconscious and it created a fresh dilemma. Or rather, it created two. The first was that we now needed to find the dead guard among all the unconscious bodies. The second question raging in my head was whether we should tie them all up and prevent the bloodshed tonight's situation threatened. When they came to, they would be spitting bullets and twice as mad as they were before. General Armand would accuse the Maharaja of gassing them: he accused him of everything else so it was a logical conclusion.

Holding my breath as instructed, and fanning the air, I stepped into the room with Jermaine by my side. Barbie came too, but the others showed better sense and stayed outside.

The gas seeped out through the open doors like water pouring through a broken dam. It lowered the height of the cloud inside the room so it was waist-high and dropping, yet I didn't dare draw a breath. There were bodies strewn across the floor which we had to pick our way between.

My pulse began to bang inside my head as I continued to deny my body the oxygen it craved. The room had to be ten metres by at least six which made it a big area to search. A table dominated the space, running up the centre of the room. We were able to use that as a focal point in our search. I slapped at Jermaine's arm and indicated the back end of the room. I'd caught a glimpse of a pile of bodies there as the white gas swirled and the farthest point from the door could be where they would place their fallen comrade. I was just guessing of course because the continually swirling mist was making it difficult to see anything much at all.

Fumbling along the table, trying to not fall over anyone who might be lying invisible on the carpet, I failed to see the form lying on top of the table until I put my hand on him.

It made me screech in fright, and in so doing, I drew a deep lungful of air.

Oops.

Jermaine saw me do it and the last thing I remember was him rushing forward to catch me as everything went dark.

A New Plan

I came to with a dry mouth and no sense of how much time might have passed.

'Oh, hey, Patty,' said Barbie, crouching to get her head level with mine. 'Are you okay? You gave us quite the fright then.'

I pushed myself upright before I committed to an answer. 'Where am I?' I was on a bed for starters, but we were in a room I didn't recognise and only Barbie was with me though I could hear voices coming through the door. 'How long was I out?'

'About two minutes,' she supplied. 'Mavis said the gas would have filled the room initially, which is why it knocked out everyone, but by the time you got some, it was all gathering near the floor so you only got a little.'

Rick poked his head around the door. 'Patricia's awake,' he shouted over his shoulder before he came into the room. 'I have to hand it to you, Patricia, that was the funniest thing I have seen in years.' Then he did a quick mime of me screaming, breathing, and falling over. When he did it, he hit the floor and his feet flew into the air which I was sure hadn't happened to me.

'This is Rick's suite,' explained Barbie.

'Did we find the dead soldier?' I managed to ask, sitting upright, and pausing in case I got the whirlies.

'You were the one who found him, Patty. He was on the table.'

So that was what I put my hand on. Deciding that I was okay, I got to my feet. 'Where is he? I need to see him.' After all that effort, I wanted to get something from it that would help me find the killer.

'Hotel security were good enough to take him away, Patty,' Barbie told me. 'I know you wanted to see him yourself, but we couldn't be sure how long you would be unconscious for.'

Jermaine and everyone else arrived at the door just as I was leaving the room and we all sort of bumped into one another. They didn't have the soldier's body in Rick's suite for me to look at, but what they did have, I saw when I got out of the bedroom and into the suite's main living area, was a pile of uniforms.

'You stole their clothes?' I blurted.

'I was just about to call the Zangrabarian delegation, madam,' said Jermaine. 'When we were in the room with the unconscious soldiers, it occurred to me that the Itarnians might not be so forward about breaking out if they were in their underwear. It ought to also dampen their aggression toward the Zangrabarians.'

'What about the armed Itarnian soldiers on their way here from their embassy? When they arrive and General Armand isn't there to speak to them, they might start shooting.'

'Hence my intention to call to the Zangrabarians, madam.' I didn't follow, but a knock at the door interrupted what I wanted to ask, and Lena came in with Rosie, Marco, and others filling the doorway.

I'd missed a few conversations somewhere because everyone was discussing a plan I knew nothing about.

'The power to their room is off and we confiscated all their phones,' Lena said. 'I sure hope this works because it's going to be everyone's jobs in the morning if they take this badly.

'Take what badly? What's going on?' I wanted to know.

Jermaine handed me the suite's phone. 'Madam, perhaps you would like to call the Maharaja in his suite? We have effectively neutralised the Itarnian soldiers. *We* have done that, not the Zangrabarians or the Swiss security at the Exclusive, and since we have no affiliation to any flag, the Itarnians cannot make this a political headache for anyone. However, the Itarnian soldiers from their embassy are bound to arrive soon and we need to be able to turn them around. I suggest we ask the royal guard to pose as Itarnian soldiers. As neighbours, their skin tone and features are exactly the same.'

'That's why you took the uniforms,' I suddenly saw what my butler had in mind. 'We show them what they expect to see: a squad of Itarnian soldiers and tell them it was a crank call or something.'

'Exactly, madam.'

Lena wore an urgent expression. 'We might not have much time, Mrs Fisher,' she wanted me to get on with it. I still wanted to look at the body, but it was going to have to wait.

I looked at the phone and then at the pile of uniforms. 'This will be easier in person. Take me to the Maharaja's suite, please.'

I knew the royal guard would be there or be nearby but explaining it and then delivering the uniforms involved an extra step we didn't need. Grabbing a bundle of clothes and boots, I stepped back so others could do the same, then we all rushed out the door.

'Don't wait for us old folks!' yelled Rick, grumpy as always. 'We'll meet you there!'

Post-mortem Bruising

W alking fast down the corridor I finally got an answer to my question about the dead soldier.

'We have him in the walk-in refrigerator,' explained Lena. 'Chef went a little bit crazy, but these are extreme circumstances.'

I'll say they are. 'He was strangled, yes?' I asked.

Lena nodded. 'Very much so, and it was some time ago, so he'd been dead for a while before they found him.'

'How can you tell?' asked Barbie.

'Post-mortem bruising?' I guessed.

I got a nod from Lena. 'There might be a clue in it, actually. The bruising shows the finger marks of the right hand very clearly. You can see where his attacker gripped him from behind because there are two distinct thumb bruises on the back of his neck, and all five digits of the right hand show up, but there are only two bruise marks from the left hand as if the killer is missing fingers.' She then adjusted her armful of clothing so she could hold up her left to show what she meant. The index, middle, and ring fingers were folded down as if the fingers had been amputated at some point in the past.

'Do we know of any guests, or staff I suppose,' I added as it occurred to me to include them, 'with missing fingers on their left hand?'

I looked around but got blank faces from everyone. It was a clue, but it was only of any use if we could use it to find the person responsible. I doubted the ambassador's killer was Martha, I never really pictured her as the killer but even if she had stabbed the ambassador, I doubted she was strong enough to overpower and strangle the Itarnian solider. I still wanted to find her, but if she hadn't killed the ambassador, why would she kill the soldier?

'There's one other thing,' Lena said, sounding uncertain for once. 'It's probably nothing ... but, well, he was wet.'

'Wet?' I echoed.

'Yes, madam,' replied Jermaine. 'His clothing. Not all of it, but the cuffs on his tunic, and around his waist and groin were soaked. It was as if someone had thrown a bowl of water at him or hit him with a short burst from a fire hose.'

Why would he be wet. I felt the bundle of uniform I carried. It was bone dry. 'Has anyone else got a damp uniform?' I enquired but got a chorus of negatives in return.

Thinking about the uniforms reminded me of General Armand and the rest of his men now in their underwear. Swinging my head around until I could find Agnes, I asked, 'How long will that gas keep them unconscious for?'

'Not very long,' she tried to look at her watch but with an armful of clothes, all she succeeded in doing was dropping a boot. 'Um, they will be out of it by now I should think. It's been more than fifteen minutes.'

'Did you just leave them where they were?'

It was Lena who answered my question. 'I locked them in the room. It won't hold them forever, I'm sure, but if it delays them a short while and we can deal with the squad from their embassy, then maybe we can get back to working out who killed the ambassador. I left guards outside the room so we'll know when they break free.'

It was enough for now, and we were at the elevator already. Squeezing tightly together, we all got in and rode it to the top floor where we were met by two members of the royal guard. They were on high alert, poised, and ready for the Itarnians no doubt, but they recognised me instantly and relaxed.

'Mrs Fisher, the Maharaja is expecting you?' one asked, a confused tone to his voice.

The entire upper floor of the hotel was dominated by a single suite which might be more accurately described as a palace looking over the London skyline. The elevator opened into a lobby which was the only space on the top floor that was not inside the suite.

'He is not,' I told them. 'However, it is imperative that I speak with him now.' Then the man noticed the uniforms in my arms. 'Imperative,' I reminded him.

With a crisp nod, he moved to the suite's door where he spoke quietly enough that none of us heard what he said. The door opened a crack and then swung wide as the guards inside took stock of the mishmash group facing them. For a second, I thought they were not going to let me in, but Aladdin appeared, his head popping up behind the line of guards facing us as he forced his way through.

'Mrs Fisher, so good to see you. Have you news to deliver? The Maharaja will be so relieved to hear from you.'

'Hello, Aladdin. I'm afraid I am not here to reveal the identity of the ambassador's killer. I wish I were. Instead, I must beg the Maharaja's indulgence as I borrow his royal guard.' Aladdin didn't understand what I meant but he led me inside with my trail of friends following behind.

The Maharaja's rooms on the top floor of The Exclusive were a whole new level of luxury. It was like stepping into the world's most expensive spa. To my left as I crossed the marble floor, the room opened into a glass enclosed garden that looked like a tropical rainforest. It even had a waterfall cascading over rocks to meet a river that then flowed away through the undergrowth.

Aladdin escorted us past the waterfall and exotic indoor garden to a spot in the middle of the room next to some couches. 'Wait here, please,' he begged as he continued onward without us.

I dumped my armful of uniforms on the couch which prompted everyone else to do the same.

'It's so pretty,' gasped Barbie, gawping in awe at the garden but also at everything else around us.

The royal guard, those members who were visible, drifted away to leave just four men standing inside the suite's front door. They were watching us, but not in an overt way where they were keeping an eye on us, they were merely observing the only other people in the room.

Rick huffed and looked around. When Agnes asked him if he was all right, he muttered, 'That damned waterfall is making me want to pee. A place this size must have a bathroom.'

'Actually, I believe it has twelve if one counts those attached to the bedrooms,' advised the Maharaja as he swept in the room with General Farhoud flanking him, Aladdin at his side, and two more royal guard shadowing his every move. 'Aladdin will show you to the nearest of them.'

'Right this way, sir,' said Aladdin, taking Rick to relieve himself.

'Mrs Fisher,' the young king stared at the pile of uniforms stacked on one couch. 'Those are Itarnian uniforms.'

'Yes, Your Highness. I'm afraid it was necessary to gas General Armand and his men.'

'They're dead!' he almost screeched in horror.

I lifted my hands as an act of defence even though there was no physical attack. 'No, Your Highness. We concocted a knock-out gas to render them unconscious. The uniforms are because ...' I didn't have the time or energy for a long explanation, so I cut to the chase. 'I need your men to put the uniforms on and pretend to be the Itarnians for a while. Can you ask them to do that, please?'

He looked at me strangely for a moment as if I had asked him to unscrew his head and hand me his spleen, but then he joined the dots and understood why. 'You mean to turn away the force from their embassy, don't you?'

'Yes, Your Highness,' I sagged with relief that he could see the plan.

Over his shoulder, he addressed the two royal guards. 'Assemble the men.' As one dashed away to alert his colleagues, the Maharaja asked me, 'This is a clever plan, Mrs Fisher. In their uniforms, the Itarnians from the embassy will not know the difference. How many uniforms do you have for us?'

I didn't know the answer to his question; I wasn't conscious when the team stripped the Itarnian soldiers. 'Actually, it was Jermaine's plan,' I admitted.

Jermaine supplied the answer. 'There are seventeen uniforms in total, Your Highness.'

We could all see the Maharaja thinking. 'I have twelve guard with me, yet I am sure that will be sufficient to fool the Itarnian embassy soldiers. It will at least give them pause to doubt their orders. General Farhoud can act as General Armand, I assume you have his uniform too?'

'Yes, Your Highness,' I replied. 'Your Highness, do any of your men have missing fingers?'

He had an Itarnian soldier's tunic in his hands which he was inspecting but looked up at my question. 'No, Mrs Fisher. No missing fingers.'

This was good news and bad. The man who strangled the Itarnian soldier wasn't among his men but at the same time, I was no closer to finding the man's killer.

As his men spilled into the room, the king ordered them to strip and change into the clothes of their former enemy and because it was their nation's monarch and leader giving the order, they all began to do just that right in front of us. Then the Maharaja himself began to strip too.

'Sire, surely you do not propose to join us?' asked the captain of the royal guard. 'It would be safer here in your suite, Your Highness.'

'The safest place for me is always wherever my royal guard are,' the young king replied.

The captain bowed his head. 'You are too kind, Your Highness. Yet I feel on this occasion, that may not be the case.'

The Maharaja paused with his hands on the ties that held up his trousers. 'Then I apologise in advance if I create more work for you. As the Maharaja it is my duty to be prepared to do that which I ask of my subjects. I will go with you and together we will win the day.' Then, having said a few words that would make his guard love him, he dropped his trousers.

Surprised by the sudden display of flesh, I spun around to face the other way. Unfortunately, there were men getting naked there too. I fumbled for a safe direction to look. 'Um, we'll just be outside, I think.' I grabbed Barbie's hand, who seemed fine with watching the healthy young men remove their clothes and pulled her from the Maharaja's suite. Jermaine, Wayne, Lena and the guards, and everyone else were already on their way out.

In the lobby area, Lena used her radio to check the guards at the main entrance.

The answer came back, 'It's all quiet so far. Hold on. This might be them approaching now.' We listened intently to the report. 'There's a series of vehicles approaching. All dark, unmarked Range Rovers.' There was a pause. 'Yes. I can see the Itarnian tags on the plates. This is them. It looks to be a dozen men. Your orders?'

Lena clicked the button on her radio. 'Do not let them in. Feign ignorance and tell them you will fetch the Itarnian delegation to come to speak with them.' The man acknowledged her instructions and cleared the airwaves.

Now feeling nervous, and telling my pulse to stop racing, I waited for the Maharaja and his men to appear. Would General Armand race to get to the lobby if all was well and the banquet was a success? Of course not. He wouldn't even go himself. He would send one of his officers and that was the ruse I hope the soldiers from the embassy would believe.

Forcing myself to take deep breaths, I slowed my heartrate and continued to wait. When the door opened a minute later, the security guards at the door were on the radio to Lena again. They wanted back up. The Itarnian soldiers outside were demanding entry and refusing to believe the story that nothing untoward was happening.

The captain of the royal guard led the way, striding from the room looking handsome and strong in the Itarnian dress uniform. When the Maharaja left his suite, I couldn't help but notice how young he looked. In his king's clothing, he carried a regal air, but dressed as a soldier, he looked like a boy in his daddy's clothes. No one was going to tell him that, least of all me.

There were too many of us to fit in a single elevator at one time, which created another delay as we waited for both cars to ascend to the top floor. The bulk of the guard went into one car while the Maharaja chose to ride with his captain, General Farhoud, and my party of friends plus two guardsmen who wouldn't fit in the other car.

Finally on the way down, the Maharaja stood next to me in the cramped space. 'Thank you for everything you have done tonight, Mrs Fisher. If you solve the crime or not, you will have done both me and the entire nation of Zangrabar a great service.'

I wasn't sure how to respond to such praise. 'Thank you, Your Highness. I only wish I was able to find a swift solution. When your royal guard have turned away the Itarnian's, I will resume my quest to find the missing persons.'

Watching the lights on the elevator control panel illuminate and go out as the car descended, I was telling myself to be prepared for this ruse to work. The Itarnians from the embassy would have no reason not to believe what they were being told by soldiers wearing the uniform of their nation.

I was prepared for it to work. I wasn't prepared for the lights to go out as the car lurched to a halt.

Trapped in the Dark

I squealed in fright and grabbed Wayne's arm where he pressed up against me; an involuntary action caused by the sudden and very complete blackness inside the elevator. I wasn't the only one to let out a shriek, Akamu did so too which instantly drew a laugh from Rick.

'How are your shorts?' Rick asked his big friend.

Grumpily, Akamu replied, 'Caught me by surprise is all.'

The captain snapped out, 'Enough.' His commanding tone and ultimate authority enough to stifle their humour. 'Highness are you all right?' he asked.

'Yes, Captain, thank you. This delay is inconvenient though. We must get moving if we are to intercept the Itarnians.'

Lights from mobile phones began to appear, shining brightly to light the steel box. We had crammed inside so that all could travel, but it was uncomfortably close and getting warmer by the second.

Barbie was the next to speak, 'Patty, are you doing okay?'

'I guess.' I wasn't a fan of being trapped anywhere, let alone in a small dark space. 'How about you?'

She actually sounded scared when she replied; it wasn't an emotion I was used to hearing from my blonde friend. 'I, um, I get a little claustrophobic sometimes. This is not a fun situation.'

The captain had his phone to his ear and was jabbering in his native tongue. From the tone of his words, I could tell he was hearing disappointing news. Thankfully, the Maharaja was good enough to translate. 'The other car is stuck as well. Captain Radan attempted to organise the men to carry on without us. It would seem fate is playing us a cruel hand.'

Barbie shuffled between Wayne and Jermaine to get to me. Seeking comfort in a friend as she attempted to quell her rising discomfort, she slipped a hand into mine. 'I don't like this, Patty. What if we are here all night?'

I saw no reason to panic yet, but that wouldn't help her. I didn't need to offer words of comfort though, Captain Radan was already getting busy. In English, Zangrabar's second language, he ordered his two soldiers to the front of the car. They were going to try to force the doors. Unfortunately, the Exclusive's policy of no weapons, meant none of them even carried the ceremonial knife that forms part of their dress uniform. Even in the Itarnians' uniforms, they would have brought their knifes along if they had them.

Patting her arm, I peered through the darkness to watch the royal guardsmen work. Jermaine and Wayne moved around so they could lend their strength to the task. So too did two of the men from Lena's security team but there was limited space at the front of the car and insufficient room for six of them to operate.

I'd seen this done in the movies, when the action star gets stuck in an elevator and pries the doors open so he can escape. All it ever takes is a little effort to get them started, but it seemed the reality was a little different.

'We're fighting against the motor,' announced Wayne a little breathlessly.

Lena clicked her radio. 'Front lobby, what is the current situation?'

A voice came back, slightly distorted by the radio waves, but clear enough for us to hear the tension in the man's voice. 'We've told them the Itarnians have been informed of their arrival and that no call for help has been sent by them. I don't think they believe us, but they are waiting, somewhat impatiently because they think the Itarnians are coming to meet them. How long until you get here?'

'Unknown,' she told him with irritation in her voice; this was the last thing we needed right now. 'We are in the elevator which has stopped moving. Both cars are frozen so we are stuck until we can get them moving again. I'm going to call maintenance.'

'That is likely to cause a problem,' said the man in the front lobby, understating the case. 'The soldiers outside are already restless. Their captain looks ready to shoot out the doors. Do I call the police?'

Lena exhaled sharply. 'No. Under no circumstances do you call the British police. The moment the soldiers outside stepped onto the steps of our building, they were no longer on British soil. You know that.'

'Yes, ma'am,' came the man's reply.

'Just hang tight. Try to reassure them that they are going to create an international incident if they storm this hotel and tell them their General and his soldiers are too busy having a great time to bother coming to the door. Give them doubt. They will have to be certain before they discharge their firearms.'

'Yes, ma'am.'

Lena's arm dropped back to her side as she ended the conversation, then she raised it again to call maintenance. 'Bernhard, it's Lena, over.' When no reply came, she said, 'He might have fallen asleep; he was due to finish hours ago. Hingis kept the team here last night to make sure everything was ready for the Maharaja's visit and he's been here all day as well. He drew the short straw because now he's locked in and cannot be replaced.' Then she tried again. 'Bernhard, it's Lena, over.'

This time the radio crackled, and a voice came back. 'This is Bernhard, over.' Rather than tired, he sounded frantic, his tone fuelled by adrenalin.

'Bernhard the elevators have stopped. There's a bunch of us stuck in them. Can you check the motor or the breakers or whatever? We really need to get moving.' She didn't explain any further, there was no need and no time.

Bernhard's response contained several colourful words before he took a breath. 'I was just about to call you, actually. I found the cause of the leak on the fifth floor, but I'm having trouble stopping it. The overflow is totally blocked up and the water has already gone through the floor. It must have got to the elevator electrics. It's probably just a short. I'll try to reset it.'

'Hold on!' Lena snapped quickly. 'Why were you about to call me? And what's causing the leak?'

Bernhard sighed as he answered. 'They are one and the same thing. The cause of the leak is a body.' He sighed again. 'I think it might be Martha.'

The news jolted me like I'd been jabbed with an electric probe. 'It's Martha?' The back of my skull itched.

Lena clicked her radio to send a fresh transmission. 'Confirm you just said you have a body there and you think it's Martha.'

'I think it's her,' he replied. He sounded despondent, like dealing with a body wasn't in his job description, but he knew no one else was going to rescue him from the task. 'I can't get to the body without going for a swim. She must have fallen into the tank. Her hair is what's blocking the overflow. It took me a while to find the problem because I didn't think to look in the tank. I know you were looking for her. I guess this is where she chose to hide.'

'We have to get out of this elevator,' I murmured to myself, and my desire got a round of agreement from everyone.

Jermaine touched Lena's arm. 'Ask him how we can get the doors open. If we are between floors, we are stuck here, but if the car stopped with a door to one of the floors partially exposed, we might be able to get out.'

Lena replayed the question.

The first thing Bernhard said was, 'That's a really dangerous idea. If the power comes back, the elevator could start moving with someone halfway in and halfway out.'

I cringed at the image. 'We have to try. Not doing anything sounds just as dangerous and maybe we are aligned with one of the floors. It could be that we can walk straight out of the elevator and onto the floor.'

Lena said, 'Give us the instructions anyway, please, Bernie. We need to see where we are.'

'There's a switch behind the panel next to the buttons.'

Wayne dropped to one knee and shone his phone at the panel while Lena leaned over with her finger on the radio send button. 'Got it. How do I get it open?'

'You need a screwdriver,' said Bernhard.

Lena huffed a laugh. 'No one's got anything like that, Bernie.'

'Don't worry,' growled Wayne, a determined edge to his voice as he ripped off his belt. With Barbie and others holding their phones up to give him light, he flipped the belt over to expose the buckle and from it, to my utter amazement, produced a multi-tool.

'What the heck is that?' asked Rick, stunned by what he'd just seen. 'Who is this guy? James Bond?'

Wayne shot a grin over his shoulder, as he folded out a screwdriver head from behind the flat panel of the buckle. 'They make you take your belt off at the metal detector, but they never check it. I had this made years ago.'

Into the radio, Lena said, 'Okay Bernie, we have a screwdriver. What next?'

Bernie's voice echoed back. 'Behind the panel there is an on/off switch. It should look like a red toggle.'

'That's it?' asked Lena.

'Yes.' Bernhard's reply make it clear he didn't see why it should be more complicated than that. 'The switch will cut the battery power to the motor. Elevators didn't used to have these but a few years back someone made a movie and well … long story short, they fitted battery power to the elevators which kicks in if the main power fails to stop crazy people trying to climb out. There were a bunch of deaths first of course.'

The panel hit the steel floor with a clang, making me jump, but seconds later, the men were back at the doors and this time they began to move. They were going to get them open, sure enough, but now I felt certain I was either going to fall to my death or get sliced in half when the elevator suddenly started to move again, and I was no longer sure I wanted to try getting off.

The doors came open, moving fast once the guys could get a better purchase. Now fully ajar and pinned there with body weight, we could all see the set of doors onto the next floor were right at the base of the elevator. We had stopped just before we would have passed whichever floor this was. Had they failed a second later, we would have travelled another foot and the gap might be big enough to squeeze through. As it was, only a child could get through.

Nevertheless, lying on their bellies, Jermaine and Captain Radan got their fingers onto the next set of doors and forced them open too.

'I can fit through that,' said Barbie.

'No way I can,' said Akamu, patting his well-fed belly.

I started to argue with Barbie, telling her about the drop on the other side. Anyone going through would come out of the elevator car more than six feet off the ground, but my words happened after the fact as she shoved off the rear wall and threw herself feet first at the gap. She slid across the steel floor and between the two men holding the doors as she made herself long and thin by stretching her arms over her head. She shot through the hole to vanish from sight. Half a heartbeat later we all heard her land lightly on her toes – her high heels were on the floor of the car next to me.

Then her head popped back up with a big grin stretched across it. 'It's bigger than you think,' she said.

'I still won't fit,' said Akamu.

'Nor will I,' said Jermaine. They were both right; they wouldn't. I might though.

Captain Radan stepped up to block the doors and I wondered why for a moment until I saw the Maharaja limbering up to perform the same trick as Barbie. 'Majesty, I cannot allow you to place yourself in harm's way like this. The risk is too great.'

'The risk of war is too great for me to consider staying in here, Captain Radan,' the young king argued.

'The nation needs you, sire.'

The Maharaja shook his head. 'Zangrabar needs a ruler who cares deeply enough about the nation and its people to put them ahead of all other concerns. If I do not do this, then I am not worthy of the position I was born into. If I go, and the elevator inexplicably moves, or my demise comes about by some other means when you are not there to protect me, then I will have died a wonderful death doing all I can for the sake of Zangrabar. And another will replace me. No person, not even a king, is irreplaceable.'

Captain Radan bowed his head. 'You are the wisest king a country could ask for, Your Highness.' I felt inclined to agree.

'I'm coming too,' I told everyone, licking my lips as my mouth went dry with terror. 'I think I can fit.'

'You'll be fine, Patty,' Barbie called back from outside.

The Maharaja positioned himself opposite the gap. 'I shall go first so that I may be there to catch you, Mrs Fisher.'

I heard him draw a breath, watched him shove off, and much like Barbie, he made his body into a spear and squeaked through the gap. His leanness of youth and Barbie's natural size zero perfection allowed them to get through, but what about me? At fifty-three, most of me was sagging as gravity took over, and though I was skinnier than I had been at the start of the year, I was a number of pounds heavier than I had been three decades ago.

In my head, I was ready, but my feet were refusing to move. 'Come on, Patricia,' I mumbled to myself.

'Are you coming, Patty,' called Barbie from outside.

'Nah,' Rick called back. 'She's gone chicken.' He said it with a smirk in his voice and that was what did it.

Even though I knew he was deliberately goading me so that I would do it to shut him up, I thrust off the back wall just as Barbie and the Maharaja had, threw myself down at the gap feet first as I put my hands above my head ...

... and got my bum wedged in the doors.

Panic set in instantly. This was literally my worst nightmare and I felt like I was lying on Madam Guillotine with her threatening to make two equal pieces of Patricia at any moment.

The doors on the floor side were the problem. Or rather, the roof was. The gap between the car door and the floor doors was less than a foot so that it made a thin slice hole like a letterbox to go through. I was just a little bit too big to fit. I knew in my head I just needed to wriggle a bit but when I squealed in fright, Jermaine and Captain Radan – the two nearest – grabbed my arms and tried to haul me back to safety. Unable to see what was happening inside the car because the skirt of my ballgown was outside the car, and probably giving the teenage monarch a great view of my gusset, Barbie and the Maharaja grabbed my legs and tried to haul me out.

The inevitable result: I was going to be torn into two pieces by those trying to help me.

I screamed, 'Arrrrghh!' But that only made everyone tug all the harder. 'Stop!' I yelled. 'Stop, stop, stop! You're pulling me in both directions at once.'

Mercifully, the tugging stopped though the hands on my wrists and ankles stayed where they were.

'Which way do you want to go, madam?' asked Jermaine.

'Let go of my arms for a moment please,' I begged. I was desperate to get myself unstuck but if I could, I was going to join Barbie and the Maharaja. With my hands free, I felt down to where I was stuck and started to wiggle myself free. That's when I discovered it wasn't my bum that was the problem; the back of my corset, which I'd worn to make my stomach look flatter and my boobs a bit livelier, had caught on the lip of the elevator. I grabbed and shimmied and twisted, and finally popped free. 'Barbie, pull me out!' I yelled and a heartbeat later I was flying through the air with a fresh yelp of terror.

They caught me between them, a hand each around my back and another to my front to keep me steady as I hit the floor. I stumbled but I was down, and I was still in one piece.

I turned back to the car where faces were peering at me from the inside. I really wanted one of the Exclusive's security guards, preferably Lena, to come with us, but she had Amazonian proportions and wasn't going to fit either.

'What about the other elevator?' I asked, 'Captain Radan, have you been able to speak with them?'

'Yes,' he called down from above my head height. 'Unlike us, they do not have a man with a secret tool hidden in his belt: they have not been able to get the panel open to switch off the motor and open their doors.'

I shot a glance at my watch. It had been more than ten minutes since we started heading down to head off the Itarnian soldiers from their embassy and the only one of us in uniform was the Maharaja who they would recognise in an instant. I needed Bernhard to help us get the elevators working again.

'Lena, where do I find Bernhard?' I called up to her.

Above us, shuffling feet resulted in her face appearing in the small opening between the doors. 'Here,' she said and dropped her radio down to us. 'I'll use another one. Just press the button and talk. You want channel six for maintenance and channel fifteen to speak with security. But don't keep it on when you are not using it. I haven't been able to go back into the control to get a new battery so it's going to run out of juice soon.'

I noted that in my head, switched it on, and tried it. 'Bernhard, hello?'

A moment later his voice came back. 'Hello, who's this?'

'Hi, Bernhard. This is Patricia Fisher. We sort of met earlier in the ground level maintenance room where they found the false electrical panel.'

'Oh.' His tone changed completely, going from a blend of exhausted yet horrified to flirty and masculine. 'Oh, yes, well I don't think I could ever forget you. Are you a professional athlete or something because I have never seen ...'

I cut him off. 'That's my blonde bombshell friend, Barbie, you are picturing. I was the old lady with her,' I told him with a sigh because I knew he would get it from that description.

'Oh,' he said, clearly disappointed. 'Oh, well, I'm kind of busy, sorry.'

I had to interrupt him again. 'This is Lena's radio, Bernhard. I know you are busy. We all need your skills to get the elevator motors running again. We need to get the Maharaja's royal guard out of the elevator cars as swiftly as possible. They are trapped inside with no way to get out.'

With a tut he said, 'I can't do anything until I get this overflow unblocked. The water is cascading down and running through the floor. It must be running along a conduit, possibly through the air-conditioning pipes because it's exiting into the elevator master control panel. I cannot fix the elevators until I fix the leak.'

Rubbing my forehead and wondering if this was a good time to question God's master plan for me, I tried to think my way through the problem calmly. 'Bernhard, can we help you?' I wanted to see Martha's body anyway. Maybe we could help Bernhard and in so doing get the leak fixed faster so he could deal with the elevators sooner. 'Tell us where you are, and we will come to you.'

Plumbing Problems

I had to argue with both Jermaine and Wayne, neither of whom were happy to have me out of sight. They wanted me to stay put, Captain Radan wanted the Maharaja to stay put, and neither of us were going to listen. There was a problem to solve and a war to avert and we were the only pieces left in play.

Ultimately, despite their concerns, they couldn't stop us, so we all promised to be careful and left them behind.

We'd landed on floor three we discovered when we reached the stairs, and Bernhard was on floor five. Heading up the stairs as fast as we could, I paused on the floor four landing when something went by the small window leading onto the floor.

'Molly?' I called as I yanked the door open. Anna and Georgie spun around to face the sudden noise with a bark until they saw it was me – Molly was supposed to be inside my suite with the door locked!

Molly's cheeks instantly flushed. 'Sorry, Mrs Fisher. I thought the dogs might need a walk. Neither of them had used that inside doggy toilet thing you brought with them so I thought there might be a bit of grass I could take them to.'

I couldn't berate her for thinking of the dogs, but she wasn't going to find any grass in the hotel that I knew of. 'Come with me, quickly,' I beckoned and held the door. 'We have a problem to solve.'

Barbie's head appeared over the railing above. She'd reached floor five with the Maharaja and was waiting for me. 'Are you okay, Patty?'

'I found Molly,' I called back, scooping Anna as Molly grabbed Georgie. Then we both double-timed it up the stairs.

Bernhard met us just outside the landing as we came out and onto floor five. He was doing his best to not look at Barbie and mostly failing as he stole furtive glances every few seconds. 'It's just this way,' he said. 'I've been trying to get someone from security to help me, but they think they've got something more important to deal with down by the lobby.' The way he said it made it clear he thought they were making it up to get out of helping him with a bad job.

Remembering that I had Lena's radio, I switched to the security channel and clicked the transmit button. 'Hello. This is Patricia Fisher. Can the guards in the front lobby hear me?'

'Front lobby. Who is this?'

'Too long to explain. I'm trying to solve the murder and I have Lena Glauser's radio. How's it going down there?'

After a pause, he chose the phrase, 'Not good,' which failed to provide any actual detail or capture the gravity of the situation.

'Can you be more specific?' I urged.

'The Itarnians have gone into a huddle. I doubt that is a good sign, but they are not currently trying to force their way in or restate their demands to be allowed in.'

I huffed out a tired breath. 'Okay, thank you.' I let the radio transmit button go, wishing I had a handbag to put it in rather than carry it the whole time. It wasn't a handbag outfit I had on though; at best I would have brought a clutch with me, the sort of bag one can fit chewing gum and a phone in.

Bernhard slowed while he fished for keys in a pocket, producing a giant bunch which he then sorted through. He'd stopped in front of a door which had the words 'Maintenance Area' on the outside. As he looked for the right key, he talked. 'Each floor has a tank to hold greywater for the toilets. It's an efficiency that was put in when the hotel was built.'

Molly screwed up her face. 'What's greywater?'

'That's water that isn't potable,' Bernhard explained, which didn't help. Seeing her continued confusion, he tried again. 'Potable just means clean enough to drink. As you might imagine, the hotel goes through a lot of water: baths, showers, and toilets for the guests and then all the laundry and cooking etcetera. Well, the water from the baths and showers can be used for the toilets and the laundry.'

'Ewww,' said Molly, pulling a disgusted face. They clean people's clothes in other people's bathwater?'

Bernhard chuckled. 'Only after it's been filtered and cleaned. It goes through a multi-stage process to remove ninety-nine percent of the impurities. It's clean enough to drink, but they add a chemical to it that makes it smell like vanilla so that people won't drink it by accident.'

'Oh, that's why!' Molly said.

Barbie frowned at the teenager. 'That's why what, Molly?'

'When I went for a poo earlier, I couldn't work out why it came out smelling like vanilla.' Bernhard chuckled again, shaking his head as the Maharaja's eyes flared in shock. Molly of course didn't recognise who the young man in the uniform was and had been giving him the eye for the last few minutes. Seeing his reaction to her unfiltered comment, she narrowed her eyes at him. 'What? Your body work different to other people's, does it?'

Mercifully, Bernhard found the right key and got the door open, distracting us from Molly's idea of polite conversation as we pushed inside.

Like the other maintenance and behind-the-scenes areas I had been in today, the lush decoration and stylish touches stopped the moment the door opened. The walls were bare grey breeze block, the ceiling exposed cable and bare light bulbs as we walked along a short corridor that took us between two guest rooms on either side. Ten yards later, it opened out into a large area filled with pipework and plumbing, motors and filters, and paraphernalia I couldn't identify. However, the standout feature was the half inch of water covering the floor.

'It's right over here,' Bernhard nodded the direction with his head, looking glum now because we were going to look at a body and the moment of amusement at Molly's antics was forgotten.

He led us to a steel staircase which led up about eight feet to a gantry around a huge tank. Barbie, Molly, and I hitched up our ballgowns, Molly and I doing it with one hand as we carried a dog with the other. Pausing next to a hatch, he faced us with his hand on the handle. 'This is it.'

'Why is it flooding?' questioned Barbie.

'That's the overflow,' he replied, opening the hatch. A waft of vanilla drifted out. 'The system pumps water into the tank continuously until it reaches a certain level. Then a ballcock,' Molly sniggered. 'A device that floats upwards with the water level, should shut off the water. Honestly, they spent millions setting up this greywater system but rather than fitting a digital sensor they use a floating plastic bulb from the eighteenth century.' Bernhard was shaking his head sadly. 'Anyway, Martha, if it is Martha in there, is caught up in the ballcock so it hasn't shut off the water coming in. And her hair has flowed out with the water going into the overflow, which should carry it away safely, but her hair has blocked it so now the water is flowing out through the emergency spill holes and causing all manner of problems.'

I peered into the gloom. Next to me, the Maharaja did the same. 'What do we need to do?' he asked Bernhard.

'We have to get the body out. The tank is too deep for a person to stand in and the body will be too heavy for one person to lift out. I knew if I went in by myself, I was just asking to drown as well.'

Wondering if she had, in fact, drowned, I put my fingers over the edge to feel the water. It was like ice. 'Someone is going to have to go in,' I said. I could see Martha, or what I assumed was Martha, floating over on the far side of the tank.

Bernhard shone a flashlight across the water, which lit the inside of the tank eerily as it bounced off the surface.

'I'll go in,' Bernhard volunteered before anyone else could speak. 'It's my job after all.'

Barbie put a hand on his arm just as he began to untuck his shirt. 'Are you a good swimmer?' she asked.

He shrugged. 'I've never drowned yet.'

It was hardly an unqualified yes.

Biting her lip in resignation. Barbie flicked her eyes. 'If you would be so kind Bernhard, please go a few steps over there and turn around. You too, Your Highness. Molly, would you unzip me, please?' Barbie turned so Molly could get to the back of her dress and held her blonde hair up so it wouldn't snag. 'I was on the state swimming team by the time I was twelve,' she told us. 'Besides, the hard bit will be hauling her up and over the side once I get her to the hatch.'

The Maharaja moved his feet instantly, backing away with an embarrassed look, but Bernhard's feet didn't look like they wanted to move. Barbie noticed he was still looking at her as her dress came free. If she let go of it, she would be standing barefoot in a pair of panties and nothing else. That's assuming she had panties on.

'Bernhard,' I prompted him.

As if remembering himself, he jolted and spun around. 'Right, yes, sorry.'

'No peeking,' Barbie warned. Both men were facing the other way, their heads looking squarely at the floor when Barbie stepped out of her dress and handed it to me. 'Hold this, please, Patty. Is the water warm?' she asked hopefully.

I shook my head slowly back and forth. 'Are you sure you want to do this?'

'Heck no,' she snorted a laugh. 'But I do want to avert a war, and I would like to get this madness done with so I can get some sleep.' She used the back of one hand to stifle a yawn, then gripped the edge of the tank, and in one fluid move, leapt up and in.

She said some choice words as the cold water bit at her skin, then kicked off to glide across the water.

Molly nudged my arm. 'Who's the pretty one in the uniform?' Molly asked me with a whisper, nodding her head at the Maharaja. 'Barbie called him "Your Highness", didn't she? Or did I mishear her?'

'No, Molly, you heard correctly. That is the Maharaja of Zangrabar. He is generous, kind, and sweet, but also the ruler of an entire nation and you should address him as Your Highness when you speak to him.'

'Is he single?' Molly asked. 'He's got a nice bum.'

I rolled my eyes, but Barbie had got to the body already. I leaned my head through the hatch. 'How's it going, sweetie?' My voice echoed as it bounced off the water and the inside of the tank.

Her own echoey voice came back with a grunt of effort attached. 'Just trying to get her hair free. I've fixed the ball cock thingy she was caught up in. It is Martha by the way.' A few more noises of concerted effort drifted out, and then I saw her face as she turned to look my way and shoved the floating body ahead of her.

Seeing her returning, I called to the men, 'Bernhard, Your Highness, I think we need your help now.'

They both dashed to join me at the edge of the tank. It was dark inside, the light shining through the hatch penetrating only the first few inches into the water so Barbie's modesty was protected as she manoeuvred Martha to the edge.

Any desire to ogle my naked blonde friend got put to one side as Bernhard got his arms into the water. He hooked them under Martha's arms and began to haul. It took all of us to get her out. Except Molly, who I sent away with the dogs since they were getting over excited.

It was a lot of effort, and a ballgown is not the apparel of choice for such a task. Nevertheless, poor, misguided Martha came out of the tank and was laid on the floor of the gantry. Then we needed to get Barbie out, but no matter what I tried, I couldn't help her clamber up the smooth sides of the tank and there was nothing for her to lever off.

Growling at her predicament and muttering, 'I swear, Patty, I don't know why I bother with clothes some days,' she called to have the men help her.

The Maharaja dutifully kept his eyes closed tight while he helped the naked woman escape the frigid water; he was an absolute gentleman. Bernhard not so much.

I helped Barbie back into her dress, which would do little to warm her up, but was the best I could do. Then I crouched to examine Martha.

'She's been stabbed,' the Maharaja told me before I could look for myself, but then I saw it: the hilt of a knife sticking out from beneath her right breast. It had a symbol on it. As I tilted my head to get a better look, the Maharaja spoke again. 'It's my crest,' he sighed wearily. 'That's the dagger of a royal guardsman. Or rather, it's a model of one because there's are steel and that one is carbon fibre. The killer must have had it made specifically to get it past the metal detectors.'

I pursed my lips as I examined it and my skull itched again.

I took a moment to pat down her body, finding a bag in each of her trouser pockets, both of which contained more exquisite items of jewellery. 'One final fling,' I murmured.

'That's the leak fixed,' Bernhard announced. 'The extra water in the tank is flowing out through the overflow again and no more is coming in. It'll take a while for the pump to deal with the water on the floor, but I should be able to deal with the elevators shortly. I just don't want to try turning them back on while there's still water finding it's way into the electrics.'

That wasn't going to work. 'No, we have to do it now.' Bernhard looked at me. 'We need to move the elevators a few feet, that's all. The Maharaja's royal guard are wearing the Itarnian soldiers' uniforms. We need to get them to the front lobby to turn away the Itarnian soldiers from the embassy before they force their way into the hotel. That's one problem. But imagine the chaos if the Itarnians catch the royal guard still wearing their missing clothes. We have to find a way to move the elevators, Bernhard. We have to.'

His shoulders sagged in defeat as we all stared at him. He was on the spot; the only one we could look to for help at this time. 'All right, there might be something I can do.'

The Maharaja slapped him heartily on the shoulder. 'That's the spirit. A keen mind and a will to succeed can overcome any obstacle.'

'Okay, okay. We need to go down one floor. That's where the water is entering the elevator breaker box I think, though goodness knows how it is getting there. It must have found a way through the AC system or something. That's the thing with these buildings: you never know what problems might occur until they do.

I wasn't ready to go yet. Giving up on trying to keep my stupidly expensive dress dry and clean, I knelt in the puddle of water next to Martha. 'I need to see the knife,' I let everyone know what I was doing before I grabbed it. I was ruining the chance to lift a set of fingerprints, though I felt certain there wouldn't be any, but I did so because I needed to answer a question.

With my left hand braced against her chest, I wrapped a layer of my dress around the blade before grasping it, then yanked it free, the wound making a squelching, sucking noise as it moved.

Molly said, 'Ewww!' again and gave a full-body shudder.

The knife had a wickedly sharp blade to one side and ridges on the other. Quite what the purpose of the ridges might be I didn't know and never wanted to ask. It wasn't the same type of knife the killer used to stab the ambassador though. Not according to Wayne Garrett, at least, and I believed him.

Barbie and the Maharaja moved in next to me. 'What do you see, Patty?' Barbie asked.

I put the knife down. Laying it in the water next to her body. The special investigators from Switzerland would undoubtedly take offense at the evidence being tampered with, but I didn't care too much about that. Standing, I said, 'We have more than one killer.' It was a bold announcement; the killer could have just switched weapons. But I didn't think so. I had a rough idea about the sequence of events forming in my mind and it fit for there to be more than one person behind the deaths tonight. My picture of events had gaping massive holes in it though, and I wasn't sure how to fill them. To start with, the guard had been strangled by a man with three missing fingers. That person ought to be easy to find, and probably would be if we ever got a chance to look.

There just hadn't been time in the last ... I checked my watch to see how long it had been since I found out about the man with the missing finger: forty minutes had gone by. That was all. Forty minutes, and in that time, I'd convinced a king to dress his men in their former enemy's uniforms, got stuck in an elevator and escaped, reclaimed a body from a greywater tank, and now I was about to do something dangerous and probably stupid with electricity.

Time flies when you're having fun.

Desperate Measures

W e left the maintenance room and Martha's bedraggled body behind as we went in search of the breaker box for the elevator. On the way there, I passed Barbie the radio and asked her to check in on the front lobby while I called Jermaine.

'Good evening, madam. I'm sorry to report that we are still trapped in the elevator.'

I expected as much, or I would have already heard from him. 'We hope to resolve that soon.' I told him. 'The body in the water tank was Martha. She's been murdered, stabbed with a knife to the heart and it was made to look like the killer was a member of the Zangrabar royal guard.' I explained about the marking on the knife.

'But you believe that to be a red herring?' Jermaine sought to confirm.

His question made me think why. 'Yes, I do. It doesn't fit. I know who killed her.' I decided right there and then that I had worked that part out. The next question was why, and I thought I knew the answer to that too. However, knowing those two things didn't solve the crime or present the Ambassador's killer.

'Jermaine, sweetie, just hang tight. We're going to get you out really soon, I hope.'

'Very good, madam.'

As I ended the call, Barbie was looking worried as she listened to the radio chatter. We'd been turning it off each time as Lena advised so events going on beneath us had happened without our knowledge.

'They're going to break out really soon!' a man shouted, his voice betraying the tension he felt.

Lena spoke next. 'Stay calm, Noah. Tell me what they are doing.'

His voice came back with just as much adrenalin in it as before. 'I think they have made the conference table into a battering ram. The doors won't hold much longer.'

Lena switched from talking to him to get an update from the front lobby. 'Elias, what is the situation there?'

Elias, in the front lobby sounded no more calm than Noah. 'They have given us a five-minute warning to bring the Itarnians to the doors or they will force their way in. I'm pretty sure they mean it, and they have some convincing looking weapons.'

Staying calm and in charge, Lena then spoke to us, 'Mrs Fisher, I heard your conversation with Jermaine. How close are you to getting us free?'

We had already started running - talking about it wasn't going to get the job done quicker. Yelling as we ran, Barbie told her, 'We'll let you know,' and let the button go.

'You might as well leave that turned on now,' I shouted breathlessly. 'Whatever happens, this is going to reach a conclusion in the next few minutes.'

'Oh, God, Patty. How do we find ourselves in these situations?' It was a rhetorical question so I didn't answer, I just held onto Anna's lead and chased after her, thinking it unfair that a creature with two-inch legs could run faster than me. Molly kept pace easily, Georgie running excitedly in front of her until we reached the stairs. There we had to scoop the dogs; their legs are too short to negotiate the steps going down.

One flight down, the dogs hit the carpet and took off again, chasing Bernhard, Barbie, and the Maharaja as we raced to save the day.

Skidding to a stop, Bernhard began fiddling with his huge bunch of keys again, jangling and juggling them to find the right one.

'This is the door?' asked Barbie.

Bernhard didn't look up, but said, 'Uh-huh.'

While I did my best to not bend over double from breathlessness, my blonde, gym instructor friend, took two paces back then shot forward and kicked the door off its hinges.

Molly used several expletives in awe and Bernhard dropped his keys, but we were in and Barbie had hold of Bernhard's shirt as she dragged him through the gap and over the door now lying on the floor.

'Come on, Bernie,' she encouraged. 'You've already had the reward of seeing me naked. Now it's time to earn it. What magic trick have you got to turn the elevators back on without electrocuting yourself or anyone else?'

I picked Anna up once more and got Molly to carry Georgie as we followed them inside. My eyes were peeled for pools of water, my terror up a notch as I imagined the water making its way through the ceiling and into the elevator breaker panel to then create an electrified floor.

There was nothing like that, but we could all see the one breaker box which the water had got to. It sat on the wall opposite us as we came in and had the words 'Elevator Main Buzz B' written on a sign above it. About five feet above that, a large diameter pipe dripped water directly onto the top of the panel where it then ran down the cable sprouting from the bottom of the panel and followed them into the floor. Given the amount of water we'd seen in the room with the greywater tank, I found it surprising more systems hadn't been affected.

'Is that safe to touch?' asked the Maharaja, watching the water dripping onto the electrical panel.

In response, Bernhard walked up to it and flipped it open. 'Yeah,' he snorted a wry laugh. 'It's just not safe to be near when we turn it back on.'

'Why not?' asked the young king.

Bernhard took a step back and scratched his head as he looked about the room. He was searching for something, bobbing his head to look in corners and underneath the equipment in the room. In a distracted way, he said, 'Because the water is forming a short between the circuit we wish to activate, and every other circuit in the panel. Including directly to earth. When I hit the breaker to pull live electricity back into it, the chances are high that the panel will explode.'

'Explode?' repeated Molly.

Bernhard nodded. 'Kablooey! Sparks, fire, parts flying off in different directions as the breaker box reaches melting temperature over the course of half a second. Of course, it might just trip back out and we won't know until we try.'

'What are you looking for?' I asked, wishing he would tell all of us so we could help him find whatever is was.

'That,' he pointed, running across the room to where a broom stood against a wall.

Sensing what he planned, I took a step back toward the door, pushing Molly in the same direction. I wasn't sure how likely an explosion was, but I didn't want to be anywhere near it just in case.

Then the radio squawked. 'Lena, this is Noah! They're coming through. I repeat, General Armand and his soldiers are about to break out of the conference room. Do I have permission to use our weapons on them?'

Lena's response was instant. 'Negative, Noah, pull back. We will struggle to justify locking them in there anyway. Using weapons on them, even non-lethals, will be a step too far. Pull back and give them easy passage down to their soldiers in the front lobby. Out to you, Noah. Elias in the front lobby, over,' she switched from one scene of drama to the next.

'Front lobby,' Elias replied nervously. 'They look about ready to shoot their way inside.'

'Open the doors and welcome them in.'

'Belay that order!' snapped a new voice.

'Hingis? Is that you?' asked Lena. 'Hingis, this is not the time to get involved. You need to let me do my job.'

'By allowing armed soldiers to storm the hotel? Are you crazy? I won't need to demand your job after this is over, the Swiss government will have us all shot.'

Choosing to ignore him, Lena shouted, 'Elias, open the doors and get out of their way. They are coming in regardless. We have done all we can to delay them. There's nothing more you can do. Open the doors and fall back.'

As she cleared the airwaves, I took the radio from Barbie. 'Lena, we're about to put power back to the elevators! It might not last long so you need to be ready to get out if you can!' Certain she heard the urgency in my voice, I had to hope they could be ready to hit the down button the moment the power hit them.

Barbie gave Bernhard a quick kiss on his cheek and ran back to where the rest of us were standing. The Maharaja wanted to use his body as a shield, which was noble and brave of him but completely unnecessary. 'Please, Your Highness, I need you to move behind me,' I insisted.

'No, Mrs Fisher. I drew you into this and I had no right to do so. I must be the one to protect you.'

'Why don't we all just move back outside of the room?' asked Barbie, the only one among us using her brain.

'All done,' announced Bernhard.

Our eyes all swung in his direction as we stopped squabbling about who needed to be protected the most and stared in disbelief at the breaker panel. The big switch was now set to on and nothing terrible was happening.

'I might have been overly worried about the chance of a short out,' he admitted.

Then a spark flared behind him as he leaned nonchalantly on his broom, and an explosion so bright it made my eyes hurt lit the room like lighting going off.

I don't remember starting to run, but I was doing just that, bumping my shoulders against Barbie, Molly, and the Maharaja as we all ran to escape the room. Bernhard was right behind us, our group exploding back into the hallway like a blob of people all glued together.

The radio squawked again. 'This is Lena, we are out of the elevator and heading to the front lobby!'

'We're coming to you!' I shouted in reply as I was the one still holding the radio.

'This is Elias in the front lobby. The Itarnian soldiers are inside the building.' The dreadful announcement meant we were moments from General Armand escaping. He would rush to the lobby where he would find the embassy soldiers. They would rush him to the Itarnian embassy where he would victoriously announce the Maharaja's plot to have him killed or kidnapped or whatever he chose to say. If he wanted to get their countries back at war, he had all the excuse he could possibly want. How could the Maharaja defend against the general's accusations when an Itarnian soldier had been strangled, the Itarnian ambassador had been stabbed and the ambassador's aide was missing and almost certainly dead?

My skull itched again and my feet ground to a halt. Everyone else ran on, desperate to get to the front lobby where the Maharaja would do all he could to prevent General Armand from leaving.

Ten yards later, they realised I was no longer with them and began to slow also.

'Hey, Patty!' Barbie shouted. 'Are you okay?'

'I have to go,' shouted the Maharaja, starting to run again.

Molly ran with him. 'I'm going with you, Your Kingness,' she shouted, grabbing his hand to hold as they ran.

The Maharaja stared down at his hand now encased in Molly's and back at her face where she winked at him.

I took all that in, but my brain was working too fast on a different problem to really notice it. Starting to run again, I brought the radio up to my lips. 'Lena, it's Patricia, over.'

'Go,' she shouted back, very clearly out of breath.

'Has anyone checked the rooftop since you sealed the hotel?'

'No, why?' I could almost hear her confused frown.

I didn't answer her question, I doubled my pace instead. 'I'll meet you in the lobby!'

Stand Off

A s it transpired, we all converged on the stairs before we
could get to the lobby. No one was taking the elevators,
that was for certain, and I worried we might meet General
Armand and his soldiers in the stairwell. Fortunately, they
were on the other side of the building to us.

As we ran down from the fourth floor, we could see and
hear Captain Radan and everyone from his elevator on the
stairs a floor beneath us. Actually, it was Rick I heard first,
complaining about his knees as he descended as swiftly as his
body would allow. I knew Akamu would be keeping pace with
him, but I figured if the two old Hawaiians were there, then so
too was everyone else.

'Jermaine!' Barbie called, racing ahead, and taking each flight
of stairs in a single jump because her legs were made of
rubber.

Jermaine's head appeared ten feet below me, his head poking out to look up. I managed to shoot him a wave, but I didn't expect them to wait for me. I was the rear-guard, going slower than anyone else as the younger legs raced for the bottom.

I caught up to Rick and Akamu who were with Agnes and Mavis, the two women choosing to slow their pace and not leave the men behind. I had too little oxygen left in my body to say anything and my hands were full of dachshund, radio, and a bundle of my ballgown to stop me tripping over it as I ran.

I hit the bottom flight of stairs to find everyone gathered just inside the door to the front lobby. Captain Radan and Lena Glauser were peering through a crack in the door. They were watching whatever was going on outside and keeping quiet.

It was only when I reached the back of the group, that I realised how few people there were. I expected to see the royal guard. 'Are the others still trapped in the elevator?' I asked with a whisper.

Wayne, standing just a few feet away, nodded his head. 'Their elevator descended but the power cut out before they could get the doors to open and they still don't have a tool to open the panel.'

It was neither good news nor bad news at this stage. We were way past the point where a show of force was going to achieve anything. I pushed my way through the press of people to get to the front where I found the Maharaja, General Farhoud, Barbie, Jermaine, and Captain Radan, plus Lena and Rosie.

'Lena are you still armed with your taser thingy?' I asked. She lifted the bottom hem of her jacket to show it in a pouch on her belt. 'Can you take it out please?' While she fiddled with the pouch on her belt, I passed Anna to Jermaine. He wasn't expecting her, but as my self-appointed butler, he was always ready to perform any task I required of him.

'Here comes General Armand,' hissed Captain Radan.

'We need to act now,' insisted the Maharaja.

'And we will, Your Highness,' I assured him before leaning in to whisper quietly in his ear. When he nodded his understanding, I straightened up, looked down at my ruined dress with a sigh and accepted my fate.

Placing a hand on the door handle, I said, 'You too, Rosie. Get your team to take out their weapons and follow me, please.' If anyone was going to question why I was giving orders, they never got a chance to because I shoved the door open and walked through it.

From the opposite side of the front lobby, General Armand was leading his soldiers from another stairwell. There were maybe thirty yards between us, and on a forty-five-degree vector between us were the Itarnian guards from the embassy.

'Well done, gentlemen,' called General Armand, his tone full of praise. 'You have rescued your fellow soldiers and a grateful general from the clutches of our treacherous neighbours in Zangrabar.'

The embassy soldiers, in their combat fatigues looked at the general but appeared startled to see a body of men advancing on them in nothing but their underwear. However, my appearance followed by others streaming out behind me split their attention and added confusion.

Their weapons sprang up and into their shoulders as they aimed them at us, the threat obvious until they saw Captain Radan striding toward them wearing the dress uniform of their own army. I could imagine the conflict in their heads. They were sent to rescue a body of their countrymen, but who was who?

In response, their captain barked an order to divide his force. A heartbeat later, half his men had their weapons trained on General Armand as well.

The general's face went purple. 'What are you doing? Don't you recognise me? I am General Armand, Commander in Chief of Itarnia's combined forces. Order your men to lower their weapons right now!'

The captain of the embassy troops held his ground. 'If you are General Armand, then who is that?' He pointed to General Farhoud, emerging now from the crowd of people behind me. General Farhoud was wearing General Armand's uniform and carrying it off perfectly.

It was time for me to end this. 'I believe I can clear things up,' I announced above the shouted orders going back and forth.

The embassy captain looked directly at me for the first time, but General Armand said, 'You again. I know who you are. I saw you fall off the stage at the Maharaja's coronation. What is it that you think you know about international politics and warfare, woman? The Maharaja you accidentally saved has laid a trap here for me. His peace talks were nothing of the sort. All he did was manoeuvre my country into taking a back-stop position so he could invade and dominate the ground. He arranged for me to be here tonight so he could either kill me or take me hostage and if I needed any further evidence to confirm my judgement, our ambassador is already dead, killed by the Maharaja's men before the evening could even get started.' He turned his head to give the embassy captain a hard stare. 'If you value your career, Captain, you will get the Itarnian troops out of here now. I must speak with the Prime Minister. Tonight, our nation returns to a war footing.'

I listened patiently to make sure he had every facet of tonight's events about face, and then said, 'You have been deceived, General Armand, but not by the Maharaja or indeed anyone from Zangrabar.'

My statement was enough to pause the crowd. The embassy soldiers still had their weapons raised and ready but none of them looked sure of their purpose. Most especially their captain.

Capturing the temporary silence, I made a bold announce-ment. 'The ambassador was not murdered, General. He is dead, yes, and his death was bloody, but it was not murder.'

He snorted a derisory laugh. 'What fresh nonsense is this?'

I turned my head. 'Lena, Rosie, can you toss your weapons?' The two women took a pace forward and threw their tasers to the ground where they clattered. Then emerging from the crowd behind me, three more of the Exclusive's security de-tachment did likewise.

Lena shot me a glance. 'I sure hope you know what you are doing, Mrs Fisher.'

I hoped so too. More than that, I hoped I was right. 'We carry no weapons and have come here willingly in a bid to stop the course of action you are about to take, General. As I said before: you have been deceived.'

His aide-de-camp with his terrible facial and other injuries leaned forward to speak inaudibly in the general's ear. General Armand nodded and narrowed his eyes at a point just beyond me. Then he raised his hand to jab a finger. 'That's the white whore who was in the ambassador's suite,' he accused Barbie who turned instantly red. Then he moved his arm so it aligned with Jermaine. 'And he is the man who posed as the ambassador's homosexual lover. I agree that I have been deceived, Mrs Fisher. However, it is you who has been deceiving me.'

I pursed my lips and tried again. 'It is true that I attempted to divert your attention away from the ambassador's death.'

'Murder,' he argued.

'Death,' I countered.

He narrowed his eyes and gritted his teeth. 'Assassination.'

Moving on, I continued with my policy of honesty. 'The Maharaja considered it to be too dangerous to let you know the ambassador was dead until we were able to work out what might have happened to him and who might be responsible for his death. He believed,' I tried a smile, 'for some reason that you might think Zangrabar, or the Maharaja himself could be behind such an act.'

'I do believe it,' the general sneered.

'Thus, proving his point,' I pointed out victoriously. 'Earlier this evening,' I spoke boldly and with conviction, 'a woman broke into the ambassador's suite to rob him. She posed as a member of the hotel's service staff going to his suite to collect some dirty plates. She got no answer when she knocked so she went inside and took his valuable belongings. She has been plaguing this hotel for many months, stealing the guests' jewellery, and sneaking it out of the hotel by a clever method that avoided the metal detectors which might have otherwise caught her.'

General Armand asked, 'You wish to claim that she killed the ambassador when she found him to still be in the suite? I don't believe you. This is nothing more than a clever lie to point the blame in the direction of anyone not associated with Zangrabar. Where is this woman you claim to be his killer?'

'I did not say she killed him, General. I said she was a thief and I cannot present her to speak about what she discovered because she was murdered.' My announcement got a few raised eyebrows from both contingents of Itarnian forces and I spoke to the embassy soldiers next. 'This man,' I pointed to General Armand, 'is exactly who he says he is. The men with me wearing the Itarnian dress uniform are members of the Maharaja's Royal Guard.'

'And the Maharaja himself,' said the young king as he stepped out from between Jermaine and Wayne where the two taller men had effectively hidden him from sight until now.

Now the Itarnians reacted, surging forward like starving men at a buffet and I worried I might have completely misjudged. Were they going to overrun us and kidnap the Maharaja? Just as panic began to urge my feet to run, General Armand called his men to stop.

His expression was curious now. 'Maharaja, it was bold of you to come here in person and present yourself unarmed and unprotected.' General Armand paced a little to the left and right, watching the young king as he pondered his new situation. 'My men could take you now and force your nation to surrender the land on our border. Why would you give me such an opportunity?'

When the Maharaja spoke, he sounded like a king. 'Because when faced with such an opportunity, I felt certain you would understand the impact men such as you have when you make a decision. The future of our countries lies not in my hands, General Armand, but in yours. That is my gift to you and also my penalty.' Behind the general, his aide-de-camp was whispering urgently and gesticulating wildly, but General Armand wanted to hear what Zangrabar's ruler had to say. 'I apologise for wearing the clothes of your nation. I am sure that is an insult to you, and I wish for you to believe that it was not my intention to cause affront. Far from it, in fact. This evening, I have been trying to avert a return to war, but I see now that I should have alerted you to the ambassador's death the moment I knew of it. I feared you might react by assuming I was to blame, or that this banquet was a ruse to lure you here.'

That General Armand was listening gave me hope.

'Everything that followed has happened as a result of my fear,' concluded the Maharaja. 'I only hope that we can straighten this out now and bring the guilty persons to justice.'

General Armand nodded thoughtfully but didn't respond immediately. I waited, desperate to tell him what I knew and what I believed. When finally he replied to the Maharaja, he said, 'I was told that you were wise far beyond your years, Your Highness, yet I must admit that I find myself surprised by your wisdom.' Once again, his aide-de-camp began whispering urgently, but this time the general held up a hand to quell him.

Quietly, and with just a touch of nerves in his voice, the Maharaja asked, 'Are you sure you have this all worked out, Mrs Fisher?'

Through tight lips, I lied, 'Quite sure, Your Highness.'

Now the spotlight was on me as the Maharaja took a step to his side and left General Armand's attention on me. 'Please, Mrs Fisher,' the Itarnian general invited, 'tell me who killed my country's ambassador, and my soldier, and this mysterious thief you spoke of. I am sure we are all keen to hear this mystery unravelled.'

His tone was teasing. The Maharaja's sudden appearance and heartfelt apology had given me the effect I hoped for and the room was calm. For now. If I had this wrong, the situation might end up even worse than it was before. Forcing myself to appear calm, even though I didn't feel it, I faced the room, turning slowly on the spot to make eye contact with as many people as possible. Among the Itarnian soldiers here with General Armand were several faces I might describe as hostile. They were all waiting for me to do the impossible and when I looked at Jermaine and Barbie, the best friends standing together and holding hands, they both nodded their heads at me – go get 'em.

I released a slow breath and started talking, 'When Martha Grimes, that's the thief who broke into the ambassador's suite, walked up to it, she did so because she had just seen someone leave. She mistakenly believed it was the occupant leaving. That person saw her and saw that she had seen him. It marked her for death because he knew that were she to reveal what she had seen, his entire operation would be blown. What he didn't know was that Martha was a thief. He would have assumed she was a member of the Exclusive's staff and about to find the ambassador's body. He needed to silence her but waiting for her to exit the room again, he missed his chance and had to wait for another opportunity.'

I took a breath and let my brain feel the story. Now that I was laying it out, it felt more right than it had. There were still two pieces I had to guess, but I was confident I had at least one of them right.

'Martha discovered the body of the ambassador on her way out of his bedroom where he lay bled out on his carpet. He had been dead for some time by then.'

General Armand and most of the room frowned. As spokesperson for the room, he said, 'Wait a second. You just said the killer passed Miss Grimes in the hallway when he left the ambassador's suite.' He smiled for the crowd. 'You seem a little confused, Mrs Fisher. Would you like some more time to review your theory?'

'I did not say she passed the killer, General Armand. I said she saw a person leaving the suite. She then knocked hopefully on the door and when she got no answer she went inside. The person she saw leaving the ambassador's suite was not his killer.'

'Why then do you propose, he chose to kill her?' asked the general, still believing he had the upper hand.

'Because the ambassador was already dead, and the man she saw had no reason to be in his suite. That he hadn't killed him would be moot, partly because no one would believe him if the member of hotel staff identified him as the person leaving his suite and partly because he was, in fact, sent there to kill him.'

General Armand's jaw went slack, then he threw his hands up. 'Well, you've got me, Mrs Fisher. I have no idea who the killer is, and I am fairly certain you don't either.'

Unperturbed, and starting to enjoy myself, I started on the next segment. 'You arrived to collect the ambassador a short while later. It was long enough after the man in the hallway departed for the message about the ambassador's death to reach the person waiting to hear about it. The man in the hallway explained about the woman who had seen him and received fresh instructions to deal with the threat she posed. She couldn't be allowed to live; the person behind this plot has been playing international political warcraft and to be caught now would ruin all he hoped to achieve. In the time that elapsed, Martha found the ambassador's body and screamed, drawing me from the suite opposite. The Maharaja left the banquet to collect his guest of honour but found me and my friends in the ambassador's suite. He asked me to find the killer, hoping that by presenting you with why your ambassador lay dead on his carpet, he might prevent the natural conclusion you instantly drew.'

General Armand had the decency not to argue.

'The subterfuge with my two friends and one of the Exclusive's own security guards,' I pointed out Rosie, 'was my idea. In fact, all the lies told to you tonight were mine and nothing to do with Zangrabar at all.

'They are wearing my uniform,' he pointed out.

'Which my friends and I took from your unconscious bodies after we gassed you. The Maharaja and his royal guard were never involved and knew nothing of our actions.' I wasn't certain he believed me, but it wouldn't matter by the time I was done.

'You are yet to reveal who killed the ambassador, Mrs Fisher,' he growled.

'Yes, I am,' I replied brightly as if thanking him for making that important point. 'Martha couldn't tell anyone what she had seen because she is employed here as a chef. As such she would have no excuse for being on the guest floors, but she is an accomplished thief, and recognising that the game was up – I'd seen her face, and the Exclusive's security team were asking questions – she went on a final burglary spree, getting all she could before she would leave the hotel for the last time. Had she been less greedy and left straight away, I might never have solved this crime. As it is, her murder left me with no doubt as to the identity of her killer and the man she fatefully passed in that hallway.'

'So, who was it?' General Armand demanded to know, his impatience getting the better of him.

I was completely in charge now; they were all hanging on my every word. 'Martha's body was discovered in a greywater tank on the fourth floor. Her killer found her somehow – perhaps chance, perhaps good tracking skills, but he stabbed her through the heart using the military issue blade of the Zangrabar Royal Guard and then left it in her chest for us to discover.' I paused and let that sink in for a second. 'Did you notice anything unusual or peculiar about your soldier? The one who was killed this evening?'

'I noticed he was taken from us when we were gassed and locked in that room. I want his body returned to me for proper burial,' he growled again. He didn't like that I was controlling things, that much was obvious.

'I am sure that will be arranged, but it was important that we had the chance to examine him. You will remember I begged you for that earlier this evening. There were two things you should have noticed, General Armand. The first was that the front of his tunic and the sleeves were wet. The second, was that he smelled a little of vanilla.'

He looked about to see if any of his men had any idea what I was talking about. 'Is that right?' he asked. Several of his soldiers nodded.

'The Exclusive recycle the bath and shower water for use in the toilet cisterns and laundry. It is filtered and stored in greywater tanks.' I let that hang and watched as people began to see the connection.

General Armand screwed his face up. 'You want me to believe one of my soldiers, a private by the way, was here tonight to hatch a plot to return our two countries to war? You wish to convince me that he went to kill the ambassador, who was already dead according to you, and then found and killed a woman who he believed might identify him?'

I nodded. 'Yes.'

He snorted a small, wry laugh. 'Then pray tell me, Mrs Fisher. Who killed him? Did he strangle himself out of remorse?'

'Who suggested you look for the ambassador tonight, General?' I asked him and watched his eyes for the flicker of movement I knew would be there. I didn't breathe in the seconds before I asked, nor as I waited for his reaction. If I was wrong now, I was sunk.

But I wasn't.

'Who has been telling you that Zangrabar cannot be trusted and has lured you here to kidnap or kill you?' This time, his eyes didn't just flicker, they lingered, and he turned his body to look at his aide-de-camp.

When the general looked at him, so did everyone else. 'I am sure he believes he has good reason to want the war to resume and I am sure it will be revealed when we question him. The reason does not matter, only that he sent your soldier to kill the ambassador, then ordered him to find and kill Martha, and finally strangled the soldier as he always planned to do. With the solider dead, he could point the finger at Zangrabar for the ambassador's death and who could say otherwise. Leaving him alive exposed the possibility that he might crack when questioned or slip up and talk to the wrong person.'

'But you told us the ambassador was already dead,' murmured General Armand as he continued to stare at his aide-de-camp.

The aide-de-camp held up his wooden hand. 'You believe I can strangle a man with one hand. A strong, young man at that? Was there evidence that he had been knocked unconscious first? A large lump to his skull perhaps?' He was throwing doubt on my accusation and his general swung his gaze back to me.

'Postmortem bruising showed the strangler had three fingers of his left hand missing.

The aide-de-camp held up his false left hand as a demonstration.

'Take it off,' I demanded.

His eyes flared in panic. 'Yes, Amir, take it off,' General Armand added his order to mine.

The aide-de-camp took a step back. 'Sir, I ...' he backed away another pace, but then he was seized by the Itarnian soldiers, who came from behind him as a crowd, overpowering him easily. I didn't need the false hand to come off to know what we would find beneath it, but I watched to satisfy myself anyway.

His left hand was a mess, just like most of the rest of him. Without his uniform on, we could see the scarring that covered a good portion of his body. 'They did this to me!' he raged as the soldier held his mangled hand out for all to see. 'They did this,' he repeated, this time with a sob, 'and you were ready to retire and live a peaceful life, my general. It was your job to lead us to victory!'

'Lower your weapons.' General Armand gave the order to the embassy soldiers who looked utterly relieved to be able to relax.

The Maharaja walked forward, passing me to cross the space between the two groups. When he reached the Itarnian general, he bowed deeply from the waist. When he straightened once more, he said, 'Together, our two nations can find a peace that will last for all time. We must all forgive the sins of the past and look for a future where our children's generation know not what there ever was to fight about.'

General Armand bowed equally as deeply and when he straightened, he extended his hand to the Maharaja. 'It will be my honour to be a part of that new future, Your Highness.'

The occupants of the front lobby were watching the two men meet and exchange words which looked set to guarantee a prosperous future for both nations. It was an historic moment, but the moment they finished, and their handshake ended, all eyes, including theirs, turned back to me.

'Mrs Fisher,' prompted the Maharaja. 'I believe you promised to reveal the identity of the ambassador's killer. We now know what happened to General Armand's soldier, and to the thief, but if neither they nor the general's aide-de-camp killed the ambassador, who did?'

I let my shoulder slump a little for it was nearly over, yet I kept my eyes on the Maharaja when I announced, 'For that, I'm afraid we need to go to the roof.'

The Ambassador's Killer

W ith the elevators out of action, the journey to the roof was not a short or swift one. Only Barbie approached the challenge with glee, smiling at me as she bounded up flight after flight, pausing on each landing for me to catch up. I could hear Rick and Akamu complaining about having to go back up having gone down only a short while before. I knew they weren't curious enough to get all the way up twelve floors and then one more to get to the roof, and smiled to myself when I heard them get off on the second floor to head back to the banquet.

Now that hostilities were at an end, the banquet might even resume, I told myself, and that made me think about having a gin and tonic as a reward.

Who was I kidding? I was going to have three.

Up and up we went, climbing flight after flight of stairs. The Maharaja, General Armand, Barbie, Lena, and more besides, all pressed me to tell them why we were going to the top of the building, yet I remained enigmatically silent on the subject. Dragging fifty people with me, I had a minor tremble of terror that I could be wrong, but I had committed to it now and it was the only thing that made sense.

Carrying Anna under one arm, I paused on the tenth landing to give my legs a break. Caught my breath, then pushed on. Finally at the top, I found Lena waiting for me with her radio. The door had been locked electronically from the control room when they sealed the hotel. All she had to do now, was transmit the order to unlock it.

'What is it that you expect to find on the other side of this door, Mrs Fisher?' she asked.

I really wanted to ask why no one else had managed to work it out, but to do so would be arrogant and rude. Instead, I gave her, and anyone within earshot, a cryptic reply. 'The ambassador's killer.'

Lena paused with the radio by her lips to see if I had anything more to say, then pressed the button and said, 'This is Lena. Open the roof door.'

I heard a solenoid click inside the door mechanism and the final moment of truth had arrived. All eyes were on me at the end of the landing that led to the roof. There were people stacked up waiting to see what this was all about, and they spread down the last flight of stairs there were so many of them. Poised to go onto the roof, it was silent save for the sound of laboured breathing.

Facing the crowd, I said, 'The ambassador's death was an accident.' My statement was met with sceptical looks, raised eyebrows, and one or two comments I didn't hear but imagined were most likely derogatory. 'Agent Garrett?'

From the middle of the crowd, a hand raised. 'Here, Mrs Fisher.'

'Agent Garrett you inspected the knife wound to the ambassador's chest, correct?'

'Yes, indeed, Mrs Fisher.'

'Can you describe it, please?'

Now on the spot, he fumbled his words for a second before stopping and starting again. 'The knife was a dagger with a blade on each side. I wasn't able to gauge depth, but four to six inches would be my guess. The blade itself was about half an inch wide.'

'Thank you, Agent Garrett.' General Armand was at the front of the line of people facing me, his eyes finding mine when I looked his way. 'You made your thoughts on homosexuality clear earlier this evening, General. It is still outlawed in your country, is it not?'

'It is,' he replied without giving further comment on the subject.

'Have you wondered where the ambassador's lover is?' I let the question hang.

Barbie tutted at herself. 'Dang it. I forgot about him.'

Turning around, I pushed the rooftop door open to gain access to the roof. It was a wide flat expanse for the most part. The flatness was broken up by the stairwell we were now exiting from, several antennae poking up next to a large satellite dish, and a large air-conditioning plant.

With people filing out behind me, I called as loudly as I could, 'Behrouz Parastui.' I waited for an answer, then repeated myself. 'Behrouz Parastui, please show yourself. I know the ambassador's death was an accident. I know you came up here to kill yourself, but that is not what he would have wanted, is it?'

A small movement to my left caught my eye as the man stuck his head out from behind the air-conditioning plant, saw the swathe of people, and ducked back again.

Terrified that we might spook him, I put Anna on the floor and took Georgie back from Molly. 'Can you all please wait here for a moment?' I didn't think they would, but with the Maharaja requesting people do as I asked, I was able to advance by myself.

Hiding behind the air-conditioning system's giant air intake, a shrivelled miserable form of a man sat crouched and huddling himself. He glanced up as I rounded the corner with my dogs leading the way, 'It's just me,' I told him. 'You gave us all quite the scare.'

'It wasn't my fault,' he sobbed.

'Tell me how it happened,' I begged, lowering myself to the floor in my expensive dress. It was already ruined; there was no point in trying to save it now.

The wretched man sobbed and snivelled and told me the story I expected to hear. When he just couldn't be found in the hotel and I remembered asking about the killer escaping by the roof with a paraglider or something, I learned it was also locked like the ground floor exits and dismissed the notion. It was only later, when I couldn't make the murder fit any of the other players, that I reconsidered the roof and that was when it hit me. Yes, it was locked, but they locked it more than an hour after the ambassador died. We knew Behrouz hadn't left the hotel and he couldn't be found in it, which only left one place he could be. Imagining a scenario where he was on the roof, led me to question why, and the rest of it fell into place.

He and the ambassador were planning an afternoon in bed. The suites were private, and it is a luxurious environment for two lovers to enjoy together. As the ambassador's aide, he laid out his jewellery and clothes and unpacked his bags. Then, he took out the ambassador's mail to open and sort.

He didn't get to it right away; the ambassador called him from the bedroom, but an hour later, after he'd showered, he went back to the desk to tackle the mundane task and was surprised when the ambassador appeared behind him asking, 'How do I look?'

Behrouz spun around with a letter in both hands and the letter knife sticking out. An ordinary thing to do, but the ambassador was already throwing his weight forward to wrap his young lover in a hug and the knife went straight through his heart. Horrified, Behrouz watched as his lover fell to the carpet, clutching his chest as blood flowed out around the knife. Panicking, Behrouz pulled it from the ambassador's chest, which made things worse, and the ambassador died just a few minutes later.

Naked and terrified, Behrouz was inconsolable but there was no one to console him anyway. Their love was forbidden in their home nation, labelled as a sin, and treated with contempt. Knowing he would either be charged with murder or have to reveal the truth about their relationship only to be disgraced and condemned anyway, he chose to end his own life.

Homosexuals did not do well in the jails of Itarnia but high up on the rooftop, he hadn't been able to find the courage to jump.

'It's going to be okay,' I assured him. 'They will believe what you say. Do you still have the letter-knife?' From his jacket, he produced a thin, two-sided blade that looked like a long stiletto knife. It still had blood on it.

I levered myself off the dirty rooftop and offered him my hand. 'Come along, Behrouz. This will be tough, but it will be okay.'

He let me lead him around the air-conditioning unit and back into sight where the crowd of eyes staring at him must have made him feel terrible and afraid. His hand tugged at mine a little as his feet faltered, but he let me lead him on.

People parted as we neared, until I reached Lena. 'This is Lena Glauser,' I told Behrouz. 'She is head of security here at the Exclusive. There are two special investigators due to arrive very soon. They will need to take a statement from you. Give them the letter-knife and tell them exactly what you told me.'

He met my eyes, showing me how haunted he looked. There was nothing more I could do for him, but I was sure he would be all right. He needed time to process his personal grief which he wouldn't get any time soon, so I gave him a tight smile and let his hand go.

The crowd parted as Lena led him through them, the security team falling in behind as they took Behrouz away.

I was weary and hungry, but it was done. The special investigators were bound to want to talk to me, but that could wait a while. I was going back downstairs to find myself a drink.

Oh, yeah. The stairs. Now I've got to go all the way back down them.

Getting Reacquainted with Some Old Friends

Twenty minutes later, my very good friends, gin and tonic, arrived courtesy of my butler, Jermaine. He knew me well enough to bring two glasses and the first one didn't last very long as I got reacquainted with them.

Placing her own empty glass back on the table, Barbie wanted to know, 'How did you work out about the letter-knife, Patty?'

It was a good question and I gave her an answer. 'On the desk in the ambassador's office was a pile of mail. Some were opened and some were not, indicating the task of opening them was part done. The tops of the envelopes which had been opened were slit, not torn but there was no letter-knife in sight. The type of blade that killed the ambassador is exactly the type of blade one gets on a typical letter-knife. It took me hours to work that out, I don't know why I didn't see it sooner.'

She accepted my answer but wasn't done yet. 'But how did you know the general's aide-de-camp had part of a hand left under his false hand?'

I gave her a shrug. 'I guessed. It had to be someone, and he was the only one whose hands I couldn't see.'

'You guessed,' David snorted. He joined us the moment we entered the banquet room and Timothy Smith, the British Foreign Minister arrived soon thereafter. The event was suddenly far less formal than originally intended. The speeches were out the window since the ambassador wasn't going to give his, but none of that seemed to matter because the two generals, Armand and Farhoud, were sitting together and sharing stories as if they were old friends.

We were back in the banquet room with a full room of people. The hotel staff had hurriedly gone door to door throughout the hotel and invited all the guests back. Fresh food was brought out, drinks were ferried from the bar and empty glasses taken away, and the evening was becoming a success despite the double murder and one accidental fatal stabbing.

Not all the guests had returned to their seats, some electing to stay in bed, or just get a cab and escape no doubt, but their absence meant we could combine tables and swap seats so the Hawaiians with their con artist, criminal girlfriends came to join us and we were able to have a great time talking about our escapades aboard the Aurelia.

When a lull in the conversation occurred, David leaned to Timothy and asked, 'Do you think you might present me to the Maharaja, old boy? I'm really keen to get a picture with him for my collection.'

'Of course, David,' chuckled the foreign minister. 'I really ought to be getting back there, truth be told. I helped them broker this peace after all; it would be wrong for me to now avoid them all night.'

'I shall not be long,' David assured me, but I got to my feet as well.

'I'm coming with you actually. I have a big favour to ask the Maharaja.' Barbie frowned at me, curious about what the big favour might be, but I wanted no one to know. It was more likely to succeed that way.

We returned to our table a short while later and conversation drifted along. David wanted to know where I was going to be since he knew I was going away and didn't know when I would be back. I did my best to be polite when I refused to tell him anything. We had been on a couple of dates and he was nice to be around. Under different circumstances, like when there wasn't someone trying to kill me and anyone associated with me, I might have fallen for him.

I expressed that I would see him when I returned and only after doing so did I realise that I had yet again given him hope of something in the future. Feeling far too tired to deal with this now, I knew I needed to. Reaching forward to the table, I took his hand.

'David.'

'Yes, Patricia,' he was keen to hear what I might say.

'I want you to forget about me. I know you think there can be a future between us, and I am not saying it could never happen, but it would also be wrong for me to allow you to wait when there could be someone for you whose life isn't the mess mine is right now.'

'I think of you as a rare flower, Patricia,' he said as plainly as he could. Looking directly into my eyes, he told me, 'Such things bloom rarely, Patricia, and sometimes all one can hope for is to be there when they do. Patience is required, so if it is patience I must employ in order to be there when you bloom, then I shall consider it a small price to pay.'

Honestly, I felt like weeping. Alistair Huntley swept me off my feet with his handsome face and position of power, but that happened at a time when I felt vulnerable, scared and alone. No one had ever spoken to me the way David just did. It felt like poetry a person might have spent many hours trying to craft, yet it was just the man speaking directly from his heart.

I was more confused than ever, and he could see it.

Gripping my hand in both of his, he said, 'Patricia, I am going to leave in just a moment. I have an important meeting in the morning. I want you to go where you are going. Do what it is you have to do and then return home safely. I will be waiting for your answer.' Then he bent his head to kiss my hand and before I could respond, he was on his feet and bidding goodnight to everyone at the table.

I watched him go with a touch of sadness but knew it was for the best that he escaped the maelstrom my life had become.

None of us told our friends we were heading back to the ship the very next morning. We were flying on a private jet to Montreal where we would board a smaller private jet to get us to Nova Scotia where we would find the ship waiting for us.

After the excitement of tonight, I felt I deserved a rest, but I knew none was coming. The Godmother, a figure I hadn't needed to think about for several hours, was still out to get me. I could relax for now, but was the Aurelia really the safe haven I hoped for?

I doubted it. They say everyone can be bought, and if that were true, was it really that much of a leap to believe she would track me to the ship? I didn't vocalise my thoughts to Barbie or Jermaine, or even to Agent Garrett. There was no good reason to make them worry and it was possible I would be wrong.

However, in many ways, I hoped I wouldn't be. Running away to hide from the Godmother had no end to it. I would never be safe so long as she wanted me dead. I would never be able to return home, so I would board the Aurelia not to relax or enjoy a well-earned vacation, but to work out how to take her down.

I had no idea how yet, but I was going to lure her into giving away that which would lead to her downfall. On board that luxury ship, with time to think and fewer distractions, I would find a way.

I had to.

The Godmother thought of me as a helpless furry creature which she, the viper, was about to devour. Little did she know it, in fact I suspected she couldn't even imagine it, but I was laying a trap for her, and I expected her to walk right into it.

I was a little furry creature being cornered by a snake. But when the snake got close enough, when it was committed and unable to swiftly retreat, it would discover the small furry creature was actually a mongoose.

The End

Author's Note

H i, there,

    Thank you for reading my book. I wonder if this was your first Patricia Fisher escapade, which you stumbled across by accident, or if you have read them all in order and now impatiently await the release of the next book? I shall never know, of course, but whatever the case, I hope you enjoyed it; writing it was an absolute joy.

Writing a book with royalty in it exposes a need to get a few things right. How one addresses the said royal person for a start. I have been privileged enough to have been invited into Buckingham Palace, a place where few get to tread, and have been hosted by the royal family. Writing it like that makes it sound like I am a good friend of Prince William, but I confess I have never met him. Visiting Buck House, as we Brits like to call it, came about due to my long military career and I was there with many other officers.

When first presented to the Queen, the correct term to use is Your Majesty. Thereafter, in conversation, one should address her as Ma'am, which is said the same as ham. Other members of the royal household should be addressed as Your Highness and then Sir or Ma'am as appropriate to gender. I abuse that a little in this book as I have done in previous outings for the Maharaja simply because it looks better on the page or perhaps sounds better in my head.

I threw in a couple of lines about British interest in the gulf region when the Foreign Minister explains political history there to Patricia. Yet again, I chose to abuse history, but not by too much. In 2003, when my unit dug into a position just outside of Basra on the Tigris, we were at the edge of an old British airfield. The Brits were all over the region and had a major impact on the policies and politics at the time which still have repercussions now.

While I dissect the book, I feel it important to say the knock-out gas I describe is a real thing, but please do not try it at home because it is completely lethal if the chemicals used are in the wrong quantities. How do I know about this stuff and many of the other crazy things I describe?

Well, I wasn't always an author.

It's late June here in my little corner of England. Covid-19 lockdown is slowly coming to an end though I think we all fear a resurgence may occur. For now, we have some hope that life may return to a watered-down version of normality. I have barely spoken to anyone in the four months since this all started but since I only have five contacts in my phone, three of which are my mother, sister and wife, it's not been that weird for me.

I'm going to leave it at that, I think, rather than ramble on aimlessly. That's this book finished, but I'll be starting a new one in the morning and cannot wait to get stuck in.

Take care.

Steve Higgs

June 2020

More Books By Steve Higgs

Blue Moon Investigations
Paranormal Nonsense
The Phantom of Barker Mill
Amanda Harper Paranormal Detective
The Klowns of Kent
Dead Pirates of Cawsand
In the Doodoo With Voodoo
The Witches of East Malling
Crop Circles, Cows and Crazy Aliens
Whispers in the Rigging
Bloodlust Blonde – a short story
Paws of the Yeti
Under a Blue Moon – A Paranormal
Detective Origin Story
Night Work
Lord Hale's Monster
The Herne Bay Howlers
Undead Incorporated
The Ghoul of Christmas Past
The Sandman
Jailhouse Golem
Shadow in the Mine

Patricia Fisher Cruise Mysteries
The Missing Sapphire of Zangrabar
The Kidnapped Bride
The Director's Cut
The Couple in Cabin 2124
Doctor Death
Murder on the Dancefloor
Mission for the Maharaja
A Sleuth and her Dachshund in Athens
The Maltese Parrot
No Place Like Home

Felicity Philips Investigates
To Love and to Perish
Tying the Noose
Aisle Kill Him
A Dress to Die For

Patricia Fisher Mystery Adventures
What Sam Knew
Solstice Goat
Recipe for Murder
A Banshee and a Bookshop
Diamonds, Dinner Jackets, and Death
Frozen Vengeance
Mug Shot
The Godmother
Murder is an Artform
Wonderful Weddings and Deadly
Divorces
Dangerous Creatures

Patricia Fisher: Ship's Detective Series
The Ship's Detective
Fitness Can Kill

Albert Smith Culinary Capers
Pork Pie Pandemonium
Bakewell Tart Bludgeoning
Stilton Slaughter
Bedfordshire Clanger Calamity
Death of a Yorkshire Pudding
Cumberland Sausage Shocker
Arbroath Smokie Slaying
Dundee Cake Dispatch
Lancashire Hotpot Peril
Blackpool Rock Bloodshed

Realm of False Gods
Untethered magic
Unleashed Magic
Early Shift
Damaged but Powerful
Demon Bound
Familiar Territory
The Armour of God
Live and Die by Magic
Terrible Secrets

9 781739 584337